Your dress

"And the car is still intact," Jack said.

Ellie turned to smile at him, grateful for his insisting she come tonight, grateful for his understanding and most of all for his behaving as if she was the only woman in the hall.

She was with someone who could easily pass for Prince Charming, after an incredible evening.

No wonder she felt like her world had been turned upside down.

"Good night, Jack," she said. But before she could turn to the door, he'd leaned forward and kissed her. She didn't expect such tenderness. Such a light touch, a hint of what might come later. It was merely a brush of his lips against hers. Heaven help her, she wanted him to kiss her again.

* * *

Beauty and the Big Bad Wolf (SR May 2005)
Cinderellie! (SR July 2005)
His Sleeping Beauty (SR November 2005)

Dear Reader,

It's two days before Christmas, and while the streets of New York City are teeming with all the sights and sounds of the holiday, here at Silhouette Romance we're putting the finishing touches on our July schedule. In case you're not familiar with publishing, we need that much lead time to produce the romances you enjoy.

And, of course, I can't help boasting already about the great lineup we've planned for you. Popular author Susan Meier heads the month with *Baby Before Business* (SR #1774), in which an all-work Scrooge gets his priorities in order when he discovers love with his PR executive-turned-nanny. The romance kicks off the author's new baby-themed trilogy, BRYANT BABY BONANZA. Carol Grace continues FAIRY-TALE BRIDES with *Cinderellie!* (SR #1775), in which a millionaire goes in search of the beautiful caterer who's left her slipper behind in his mansion. *A Bride for a Blue-Ribbon Cowboy* (SR #1776) introduces Silhouette Special Edition author Judy Duarte to the line. Part of the new BLOSSOM COUNTY FAIR miniseries, this romance involves a tomboy's transformation to win the cowboy of her dreams. Finally, Holly Jacobs continues her PERRY SQUARE miniseries with *Once Upon a Prince* (SR #1777), featuring the town's beloved redheaded rebel and a royal determined to woo and win her!

And don't miss next month's selection led by reader favorites Judy Christenberry and Patricia Thayer.

Happy reading!

Ann Leslie Tuttle
Associate Senior Editor

Please address questions and book requests to:
Silhouette Reader Service
U.S.: 3010 Walden Ave., P.O. Box 1325, Buffalo, NY 14269
Canadian: P.O. Box 609, Fort Erie, Ont. L2A 5X3

Cinderellie!
CAROL GRACE

Fairy Tale Brides

SILHOUETTE *Romance*®

Published by Silhouette Books

America's Publisher of Contemporary Romance

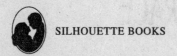

SILHOUETTE BOOKS

ISBN 0-373-19775-6

CINDERELLIE!

Visit Silhouette Books at www.eHarlequin.com

Printed in U.S.A.

Books by Carol Grace

Silhouette Romance

Make Room for Nanny #690
A Taste of Heaven #751
Home Is Where the Heart Is #882
Mail-Order Male #955
The Lady Wore Spurs #1010
*Lonely Millionaire #1057
*Almost a Husband #1105
*Almost Married #1142
The Rancher and the Lost Bride #1153
†Granted: Big Sky Groom #1277
†Granted: Wild West Bride #1303
†Granted: A Family for Baby #1345
Married to the Sheik #1391
The Librarian's Secret Wish #1473
Fit for a Sheik #1500
Taming the Sheik #1554
A Princess in Waiting #1588
Falling for the Sheik #1607
Pregnant by the Boss! #1666
**Beauty and the Big Bad Wolf #1767
**Cinderellie! #1775

Silhouette Desire

Wife for a Night #1118
*The Heiress Inherits a
    Cowboy* #1145
Expecting... #1205
The Magnificent M.D. #1284

*Miramar Inn
†Best-Kept Wishes
**Fairy-Tale Brides

CAROL GRACE

has always been interested in travel and living abroad. She has spent time in France and toured the world working on the hospital ship HOPE. She and her husband have lived in Iran and Algeria.

Carol says that writing is another way of making her life exciting. In addition to her Silhouette titles, she has also written single-title romances for Pocket Books. Her office is her mountaintop home which she shares with her inventor husband. Her daughter has just graduated from law school and her son is an aspiring actor in Hollywood. Check out her Web site at carolgracebooks.com. Her fun-loving San Francisco-based critique group can be found at fogcitydivas.com.

For the Kimpton sisters—
Grace, Ruth, Esther, Pat, Mary, Alyce and Jane
of 3040 with thanks and love from Carol Grace.

Chapter One

"Ellie, you're late," Ellie's stepmother said with a frown. Gwen Branson was standing in the middle of the Hostess Helpers office, wearing a rain jacket over her cocktail dress, her arms piled so high with tablecloths and boxes of candles that Ellie could only see her eyes shooting daggers. But she could imagine her mouth—turned down at the corners in her usual expression of long-suffering disappointment at Ellie's behavior and appearance.

But then, Gwen was *never* happy with the way Ellie looked—whether she was playing Cinderella in full fairy-tale getup as she was now, right down to the glass slippers, or wearing no makeup while on the job in the kitchen, in loose comfortable clothes with her hair pulled back from her face. Whether Ellie was late, early or on time, she still couldn't please her stepmother.

Gwen believed in manicures and facials and expensive clothes both for herself and her biological daughters. She'd given up long ago on her stepdaughter, letting Ellie do as she pleased, which suited Ellie just fine. Ellie wasn't beautiful; she'd been told that over and over by Gwen and her daughters since they came into her life. They hadn't actually said outright that she was the tall and awkward type, but Ellie got the message. At five-ten, she towered over her stepsisters, who actually envied her ability to eat anything she wanted and not gain a pound. They, of course, watched their calories and dutifully joined a fancy gym that Gwen paid for. But they seldom worked out, and even if they had they knew they would never achieve the svelte-model figure Ellie had developed late in her teens. And that annoyed them. And it annoyed Gwen, too, as she didn't want any competition for her daughters in the looks department, or any other department for that matter.

"Sorry," Ellie said, shaking the rain off her skirt. "But the kids wouldn't let me leave. They wanted to hear Cinderella tell one more story and then one more. They were so cute, I couldn't say no."

"You weren't paid to stay overtime. You were paid to run the games, feed them cake and ice cream and that's it. No stories. Because you couldn't say no, we're going to be late."

"Just give me a minute to change clothes and we can leave."

"We don't have a minute. April and May have gone on ahead to set up. The food will be there, all you have to do is put it together. I was just about to leave without you. I would have but…"

She didn't finish her sentence. She didn't need to. Ellie knew why she wouldn't leave without her, why they wouldn't cater a party without her. She was the one who did all of the hard work in the kitchen. Although she'd organized everything earlier in the day, once she got to the site she would be baking, broiling, stuffing, chopping, spreading and filling trays with her own special creations such as miniquiches and filo triangles. Meanwhile her stepmother and stepsisters would be out circulating among the guests, passing the trays, filling the champagne glasses and smiling brightly, accepting compliments for the wonderful food they hadn't made.

"Here," Gwen said, handing Ellie the boxes. "You take these. Let's go." Before Ellie could protest that she was tired and hungry and the glass slippers made her feet hurt, Gwen had turned off the lights and locked the door behind them.

Ellie drove while Gwen gave directions to an address in Pacific Heights, one of San Francisco's poshest neighborhoods. They turned into a courtyard where a valet parked their van, then helped them unload the boxes in the courtyard of the big stone house.

Ellie whistled appreciatively as they walked around the three-story building, to the back entrance while rain continued to fall steadily on her head. "Whose party is this, anyway?"

"A venture capitalist," Gwen said. "Very rich. Very eligible. This is an excellent chance for your sisters to meet him or one of his single friends. So don't screw it up." Ellie couldn't see Gwen's face, but her voice was as sharp as her pointed red nails.

Screw it up? Was she referring to the time Ellie had dropped a carton of eggs on an Aubusson carpet just before the guests arrived at an anniversary bash at the yacht club? Or the time she'd blown a fuse by running the blender, the microwave and the convection oven all at once at a fiftieth birthday party? Guests were in the dark for a half hour and had to eat crackers and cheese until an electrician agreed to a house call, at an exorbitant fee, of course.

Okay, so she'd made a few mistakes, but she was a cook, no, a chef! A graduate—with honors—of the Culinary Institute should be cut a little slack, at least by her family. But Gwen never cut her any. She had always had high standards, which were set even higher when Ellie's father died and Gwen had used the money he'd left her to start her own party planning business. The not-too-secret goal of which was to worm her way into high society so her daughters could marry well. So far it hadn't happened, but they hadn't lost hope.

Ellie was so wrapped up in her thoughts she tripped on one of the flagstones, and several plastic containers of nuts and cheese toppled onto the rough walkway. She heard Gwen draw a sharp breath, but she was spared another of her brusque warnings when Ellie nimbly scooped up the containers, which were still intact and in pristine condition. The back door swung open, and Ellie's stepsisters called out in the dark to hurry it up.

"Where have you been?" April demanded from the doorway where she and May stood waiting for them. "The guests are here. The host is fuming." She paused as Ellie and Gwen hurried into the kitchen.

Before Ellie could answer, May got a look at her outfit. "Good grief, Ellie. What are you wearing?" she asked, stifling a laugh by pressing her hand against her mouth. She and April were both in black cocktail dresses with tiny white ruffled aprons, which they thought made them look like sexy French maids.

At twenty-three and twenty-four respectively, they'd been actively husband hunting since they'd turned twenty-one, prodded by Gwen who had drummed it into their heads that it was just as easy to fall in love with a rich man as a poor one. So far, no one had turned up who was rich enough or good enough for either one of them. Ellie thought that once the girls had found suitable mates, Gwen might just pack it in.

Ellie, at twenty-six, had no plans to get married. After taking over the household duties when her mother got sick, which meant years of cooking and cleaning for her father, then for his new wife and her daughters, she was no longer interested in running a household for anyone. Not even Prince Charming. She loved cooking, but she was tired of being taken for granted.

If Ellie was ever tempted to get married, she would have to be swept away by a prince like Cinderella or Sleeping Beauty had been. She wanted passion and excitement or nothing.

Naturally she didn't confide in her stepmother or stepsisters, who would have laughed themselves silly at the idea of Ellie being swept off her size-ten feet by some prince. She'd dated several guys from the Culinary Institute, but nothing clicked. She loved kids, but in her future life as a restaurateur, she would be working sixteen-hour days and have no time for a husband and family, so it was just as well she hadn't yet met Mr. Right, if there were such a person.

"You look ridiculous," April said, shifting Ellie's thoughts back to the moment. "Who ever heard of a five-foot, ten-inch Cinderella in glass slippers making appetizers in a designer kitchen? At least we've gone to the trouble of looking our best. I guess it doesn't matter for you, seeing as you'll be out of sight in the kitchen."

"Right." Ellie slipped off her faux-glass slippers and put them in the large butler's pantry. She tied on a large white apron and looked around at the copper pots hanging from the ceiling, the wide expanse of granite counters, the stainless steel subzero refrigerator and the huge butcher block in the middle of the room. What she wouldn't give for a designer kitchen like that! Never mind, she'd have her own kitchen some day, in her own restaurant, where she'd be in charge of hiring the help. No stepsisters need apply. Just as soon as she got some investment capital, she'd make it happen. "Now where is that filo dough?" she asked.

A half hour later, she took tiny crab tarts out of the oven, then artfully stuffed little new potatoes with crème fraiche and caviar, and placed her three-cheese filo triangles on a large platter. Her sisters snatched them out of her hands and smoothly glided out the kitchen door down the hall and into the living room. Before the door closed behind them, Ellie caught a glimpse of tasteful paintings on the walls, hardwood floors, Persian carpets and tall ceilings. She heard music and laughter and a cacophony of voices. No time to think about what it must be like to be a guest at such a party. She had much too much work to do.

Ellie breathed a sigh of relief at finally having the kitchen to herself. She pulled her hair off her face and had just taken a batch of shrimp puffs out of the oven when the door opened and a tall man in a dark suit, blue shirt and red power tie walked in. Ellie was stunned, recognizing the obnoxious man who'd killed her dream two weeks earlier. He didn't have a heart, only dollar signs blazing in his blue eyes. She was so shocked to see him she dropped the pan of puffs on the floor. But when she bent down to pick them up, so did he, and her forehead banged against his. She rocked back on her heels.

"You all right?" he asked, reaching out to steady her with one hand on her arm.

"Fine." Except for flashes of light in front of her eyes and the pounding headache.

He didn't recognize her! She'd sat in his office for fifteen minutes a mere fourteen days ago. Tonight they'd banged heads, then he'd looked her over, and he still didn't know who she was! Sure, she looked like a refugee from a fairy tale, but still, she knew exactly who he was.

He was the arrogant, self-centered bastard who'd turned her down for venture capital. He probably turned down hundreds like her, every week, whereas she only got in to see a handful of men in the business of investing in start-up businesses. So while he'd forgotten her completely, she'd never forget him. He'd been so smooth, so sure of himself…and so negative.

She remembered every word. He'd said, "I'm in the business of taking risks, but I'm not in the business of throwing away my clients' money. No way would I invest in a restaurant. Do you know how many fail in the first six months? Ninety-nine percent. And even if I did invest in a restaurant, why should I invest in yours? You're not even a celebrity chef. You're nobody. You're doomed before you even start. I don't do restaurants, startups or sole proprietorships of any kind. I only take chances on ventures that have a chance of success. You don't. How did you get in here, anyway?"

That was her cue to get out and get out fast, before he found out she'd posed as the delivery person from a nearby deli, with lunches for the workers. She'd never forget that intense blue gaze, the same blue gaze he had fixed on her now.

He wrapped his handkerchief around his hand and picked up the dropped pan of puffs before she could do anything. He set it on the counter and held out his hand to help her to her feet. She felt the room tilt on its axis. Either she'd been injured worse than she thought or she was in shock over running into the one man she never wanted to see again. He, on the other hand, seemed oblivious to her state of mind and calmly helped himself to a still-hot puff.

"Not bad," he said, chewing thoughtfully.

Ellie leaned against the counter and waited for the room to stop spinning around. Her face burned from the heat in the kitchen and from embarrassment. "Not bad?" she demanded when she realized he was referring to the shrimp puffs that had won her first prize in the appetizer division of a citywide contest. Had she lost her touch? Not likely. "Have you had better?" she inquired stiffly.

He was still chewing, and he held up one finger. "I'll let you know in a minute. After I have another."

She lifted one off the pan to give it to him, but his cell phone rang at that moment, and as he spat out questions and answers about ratios and percentages and interest rates so quickly to the person on the line, Ellie found herself staring at him in awe. He obviously had a brain like a calculator. No big surprise considering his profession and his status. He ended the phone conversation just as abruptly as he'd begun, flipped his phone shut and switched gears.

He reached for the shrimp puff as if the call had never happened, and she ate one herself to test it. No, she hadn't lost her touch. The dough was light, the shrimp blended with cheese and lemon and fresh dill were delicious. If he didn't agree, the hell with him. He obviously had high standards, but so did she. Maybe he knew finances, but she knew food. And her food was always excellent, if she did say so herself.

She'd even told him so when she'd first met him at that ill-fated encounter in his office. After all, if she didn't believe in herself, who would?

After he'd demolished his second shrimp puff, he narrowed his gaze and looked her in the eye for a long moment. Here it comes, she thought. But he just nodded and said, "You're right. Very good." He stepped back to take another look at her, this time from head to toe. He looked so long and so hard at her strange outfit, at her flushed face, the wisps of hair that had escaped from the scrunchie, and finally at her bare feet, that goose bumps covered her skin. She wondered if he finally did recognize her after all. If so, did it matter? "You're the brains behind this food?" he asked.

"You could say that. I'm the chef, yes," she said coolly. As you would know if you'd paid any attention to me when I came into your office that day.

"Sorry if I startled you by bursting in here," he said. "Sure you're okay?" He put his cool palm against her flushed forehead. "You feel feverish. Maybe you ought to lie down for a while."

"Lie down?" She choked on her own words as his touch soothed her burning face. "I'm cooking for a party of thirty. *Your* party of thirty. Are you sure you think I should lie down?"

He dropped his hand. "Well, if you're sure you're all right."

"Of course I'm all right. Are *you* all right?" she asked politely.

"Fine." He frowned. "I've met you before, haven't I?" Again he gave her one of those long looks that made her feel as though she'd been stripped of her costume and stood there shivering in her sports bra and all-cotton bikinis. "Who are you?"

Ellie took a deep breath to calm her nerves. "I assume you're referring to the costume. I'm Cinderella, or I was this afternoon."

"Well, Cinderella, I'm Jack Martin and if you're waiting for Prince Charming, you've come to the wrong party. There are princes, but none of them are particularly charming. They don't need to be. They're multimillionaires. What I came in to tell you is my housekeeper's been called away tonight unexpectedly otherwise she'd be glad to give you a hand. Sorry about that.

"And now, assuming that there's been no major damage and neither of us has a concussion or memory loss, I hope it's not asking too much to get this show on the road. It's seven-thirty. Where the hell are the crab cakes?"

"They'll be out in five minutes," she said smoothly, with a glance at the oven timer. "Any other questions?"

"Yes. Are you sure we haven't met? You look so…never mind. Tell me, who are those two useless dimwits out there, Cinderella, your ugly stepsisters?"

"I wouldn't call them ugly," Ellie said, relieved he still didn't recognize her. "But they are my stepsisters."

"I asked for professional party planners, and I've got the crew from some damn fairy tale. I suppose you have to be out of here by midnight or you turn into a pumpkin."

"It's the coach that turns into a pumpkin," Ellie said tartly. "You ought to brush up on the classics."

"Yeah, right," he said. "Just as soon as I get through this week. There's a lot riding on the success of this event. But this is just the kickoff. Tomorrow we get down to business and it lasts all week—seminars and PowerPoint presentations and show-and-tell to get these guys to part with some of their millions. Food and drink oil the joints. I've done enough of these to know that. Hannah Armstrong, that's my housekeeper, will be back tomorrow to work her magic in the kitchen. All I ask is that you make an impression tonight. God knows I'm paying enough for your effort. I've got to put these guys in the mood to invest in some of my ventures."

None of which are restaurants, she thought. "All guaranteed to bring in zillions of dollars," she muttered with just a tinge of sarcasm.

"Nothing's guaranteed. It's all risky. I've won some and lost some, but I make a judgment and then I go with my gut feelings," he said. Then he braced his hands on the counter and studied her

face for a long moment. She held her breath. Yes,
he'd gone with his gut feelings about her and her
restaurant and then he'd turned her down. The temperature in the kitchen rose about ten degrees as he
continued to stare at her, and it had nothing to do
with the oven.

Jack Martin might be a money-grubbing businessman, but with his strong jaw, commanding presence
and broad shoulders, there was no denying he was
one hot man. Too bad he was rich and obnoxious.
Otherwise she'd suggest he take a look at her stepsisters. Maybe he'd like one of them. It would serve
him right, getting involved with April or May.

The tension rose along with the temperature as the
silence lengthened. She needed to get back to work,
to check on the crab cakes in the oven, but she
couldn't tear her gaze from his. She couldn't think
of a thing to say, and it seemed he couldn't, either.
She had a baguette in front of her that she was pre-
paring to slice, but she was afraid her hands weren't
steady enough to chance it. Why didn't he leave and
let her get back to work?

"I know you from somewhere," he said at last.
"Where was it, the Bartlett party?"

"No."

He snapped his fingers. "I know. You came to my
office. You're the one who wants to start a restaurant."

"You turned me down."

"Of course I turned you down. I'm a venture capitalist. I'm not running a charity."

"I wasn't asking for charity," Ellie said brusquely. "I intend to make money."

"How? Do you know how many restaurants—"

"Fail in the first six months? Of course I do. You explained to me very succinctly what I already knew. Thank you very much. But my restaurant is going to be—"

"Different. Special. I know, that's what they all say, that their restaurant is going to make it where all others have failed. Or they would say if they got past my assistant. How did you get in, anyway? I don't see chefs or any other sole proprietors. It's a waste of time."

"You made that perfectly clear. Don't worry about it." Yeah, like he was worried about her or her plans. "I'll get the money and I'll start my restaurant," she announced. "Without your help."

"Good for you, Cinderella," he said without missing a beat. "Let me know how it turns out."

Ellie pressed her lips together to keep from blurting that after tonight she would hopefully never see him again, never be subjected to further sarcasm or discouragement. Who needed it? And she was not about to tell him how she'd sneaked in to his office. That was her little secret. Instead she grabbed a pair of kitchen shears to energetically snip parsley for a garnish.

He rubbed his palms together. "Now that we understand each other, I'll let you get back to work. Shall I send the stepsisters in to fill up the trays?"

She nodded without looking at him.

So went the evening. April and May came back with empty trays, giggling and oohing and ahhing about the quality of the house and the guests.

"So," Ellie said to the two of them as she refilled their platters, "did you meet Mr. Right yet?"

"Not sure," April said. "I heard someone say David Carter is the richest one in the room. But he's short and bald. And some other guy pinched my bottom when I bent over to pick up an empty glass."

"He may not be the richest, but Jack Martin is the hottest. You know, the guy who's giving this bash. Isn't he to die for?" May asked April. "By the way, he was asking about you, Ellie."

"Really?" Ellie's pulse ratched up a notch and her hands shook once again. Fortunately she was wearing rubber gloves and she didn't drop the glass pitcher she was washing. "What did he say?"

"He said to tell you your crab cakes were excellent and he should know, since they're his favorite food and he's had them in every restaurant all over town."

"Ah," she said.

"Then he asked if you were free to do some special work for him. Why you, anyway?" May's forehead wrinkled in a puzzled frown. "I said I was available, that we work as a team, but he seems set on you for some reason. I said he'd have to ask Mom. She does the scheduling."

She might do the scheduling, but Ellie was not going to let Gwen schedule her to have anything to do with a man who thought she was a nobody. After tonight she hoped she'd never have to see him again…except for the day he walked into her hot new restaurant with his uppity friends and a high-society blonde on one arm and asked for a table.

She'd take great pleasure in turning him away. "Sorry," she'd say. "I'm completely booked, Mr. 'I don't do restaurants.'"

He'd look perplexed because he would have forgotten her *again*.

And she'd say, "Remember me? I'm nobody."

Then he'd slap his hand against his forehead when he remembered who she was and how he'd turned her down. Big mistake. Not that he'd care one iota that he hadn't helped a deserving person on her way up the ladder. Not that he'd even rejoice in the success of a plucky entrepreneur who'd done it on her own. The only thing that would bother this guy was the loss of the chance to make big bucks on her endeavor.

He'd see the crowds, he'd hear the ka-ching of the cash register, he'd see the happy customers wolfing down her specialties and paying top dollar for them. He'd know then he'd been wrong. She pictured the look on his face. Stunned disbelief. Disappointment. Humiliation. He'd pause in the doorway on his way out and give her one last pleading look. "Please," he'd say. "Let me stay. Just for one crab cake. Just one."

She'd shake her head and smother a triumphant smile. He'd walk out the door, but once outside, he'd press his nose against the window and look in. There might even be tears in his eyes. Oh, the pleasure she'd get when it was payback time.

"What are you grinning about?" May asked, giving Ellie a poke in the ribs.

"Nothing. Here you go." Ellie held the kitchen door open, and her sisters trooped back out into the rarified atmosphere of the party.

By midnight Ellie was exhausted. She could hear the guests leaving at the front door. She was packing up while April and May sat at the kitchen table drinking leftover champagne and chattering about the party, speculating about who was who and who had how much money. At least Gwen was helping fill the boxes with empty containers, because if she didn't, they'd be there all night.

Gwen yawned and said something about getting too old for this party business. But she didn't ask her daughters to give them a hand cleaning up. It was Ellie's opinion that she'd spoiled them since day one, and it was a little late to retrain them now. Oh, well, if they found rich husbands, they'd have hired help and would never have to lift a hand.

As she walked toward the van, she suddenly realized she was still barefoot and her stupid Cinderella slippers were back in the kitchen. She wouldn't go back. She might run into Him. She'd buy a new pair, ones that fit this time. As she pulled their van out of the driveway, her bare foot on the gas pedal, Ellie cast one look back at the house with its gaslights lining the walkway, and the porticos lighted by floodlights. She half expected to see Jack Martin standing on the front porch.

She wasn't disappointed that he hadn't come to ask her in person if she was available for a new job. It just saved her the trouble of turning him down. So why was she looking for a glimpse of him before heading out to the street? Just curiosity, that's all it was. She was relieved the party was over. Relieved she'd never have to see him again.

Chapter Two

Jack Martin was just as relieved. Alone at last in his book-lined study, with the sounds of traditional jazz coming from the surround-sound speakers, he could finally relax. It had gone well, so far. But he'd learned not to count on anything until he had promises and signatures to back them up. He'd been disappointed too many times in his life to ever feel totally secure. It all went back to when he was nine and his mother had walked out on him and his father. She'd claimed that Spencer Martin put his business before her and her needs. She'd said she would come back for her son, but then she married someone else—who was there for her, she'd said, but someone who didn't want to raise another man's kid. By the time she'd finally returned and tried to rekindle a relationship, Jack no longer needed a mother. He'd been raised by a succession of nannies, and he was independent and self-sufficient, thanks to his mother's absence and his father's brand of absentee parenting. From an early age he'd absorbed his father's all-work-and-no-play work ethic and had taken over his father's spot in the investment firm when Spencer had retired.

But even today his father still came down to the office, still looked over his shoulder and still gave him advice. *Never invest in a one-man enterprise. Never invest in restaurants. Take calculated risks in the office, but never in your personal life. That's where I made my mistake. Only one, but it was a humdinger.* He was, of course, referring to his marriage to Jack's mother.

After all these years, Spencer was still bitter about his wife leaving him. *Play the field, boy,* he'd said more than once. *Don't tie yourself down. Women don't understand what it takes to succeed. They want, want, want. They take, take, take.*

Jack did play the field, but not because his father told him to. It was just easier that way. Besides, what did he need a wife for anyway? Hannah ran his house better than any wife could. She was loyal, faithful, took a personal interest in his life but never interfered. Just a brief glance into the lives of his married friends and he was convinced, as he imagined even they must be, that he was one lucky guy.

As much work as he had to do, he found himself thinking about Cinderella reappearing into his life. He hadn't recognized her at first, barefoot, wearing her ridiculous costume, with her blond hair pulled back from her face. The last time he'd seen her, that day in his office, her hair was hanging smooth and straight. So smooth his fingers itched to touch it, a move so out of character for him and so inappropriate he wondered if he'd had some kind of minor brain damage.

At the time, she'd been wearing a short skirt and white shirt. From where he'd sat behind his desk he'd had a view of her long legs as she crossed and uncrossed them. Good thing he hadn't had to think of how to tell her no, because he'd been distracted by her legs and his brain definitely hadn't functioned well. Fortunately he had the answers down pat. It was a no-brainer.

Was he sorry he'd had to turn her down? Sure. Was he tempted to give her the money just because she was an attractive woman with legs that didn't quit and hair that looked like silk who believed in herself? Not for a moment. He liked women as much as anyone, but he'd never lost his head over one. They came and went, and he'd never shed a tear over any of them. He assumed they felt the same about him. He kept his priorities straight. Always had, always would.

Still…he'd wondered about her. Where had she

come from? And how in hell had she gotten in to see him when he *never* saw restaurateurs? Tonight when he looked into those soft-brown velvet eyes, it finally all came back to him with a jolt.

To tell the truth, turning her down had bothered him more than he thought it would. More than it should have. It was such an obvious decision. But even after she'd left the office, he couldn't get her out of his head. He didn't know why she'd stuck in his mind, because he saw dozens of people every week, men, women—even attractive, ambitious women— but she wasn't like the others. And yet when he'd first seen her tonight, he hadn't made the connection.

That day in his office she'd looked shocked when he'd told he wouldn't even consider investing in her restaurant. Her cheeks had flooded with color and he'd thought for a minute she was going to cry. Then she'd composed herself, stood up and marched out of his office as if she were going into battle. He re-membered standing there staring at the closed door of his office wondering where she was going next. Now he knew.

She was going back to making crab cakes and shrimp puffs for her stepmother's catering business. Seemed like a waste of talent, but what was the choice for a talented chef? Starting a restaurant re-quired a large amount of capital, and was too risky. Even for someone who lived for risks like he did. Except in his personal life, of course. But then, some might say he had no personal life. And they wouldn't be far wrong.

Before he'd had a chance to tell her that she was wasting her time that day, and his, too, she had sat on the edge of her chair, excitement and enthusiasm in her voice. Her dark eyes had been bright, a smile had played on her lips. Yes, she'd been excited about her venture, no doubt about that. But excitement didn't translate into practicality.

So she was disappointed, but at least she had another job. She was a caterer. It was probably all there in her CV. He just didn't remember. Why should he feel guilty? He shouldn't. Dammit, he was in the business of making money for his clients, as he'd clearly explained to her. Why couldn't she understand that?

Probably she'd thought he was coldhearted, just because he didn't offer her the money she'd asked for. What did she think, he'd be so blown away by the idea of a neighborhood bistro that he'd open his top drawer and write her a check on the spot? People had no idea that venture capitalists were only as good as their latest venture. That his clients depended on his judgment and that a mistake in insight could cost him a loss of his investors' confidence and maybe even his job at the firm. He told himself he didn't care what she thought or even if she understood the principles he worked under. It wouldn't be the first time he'd been branded as heartless. And it wouldn't be the last. It didn't bother him. Not at all.

He stood and stretched. He was having a hard time concentrating. Maybe a cup of coffee or something to eat. He'd been so busy working the crowd tonight, he hadn't had time to eat much beside one bite of those marvelous crab cakes. He went down the hall to the kitchen, but there was nothing left. Not a scrap. Couldn't they have left him something, considering what he'd paid for their services? He looked in the pantry, but it was empty. Except for a pair of glass slippers on the floor.

He picked them up and looked at them. "You left your slippers, Cinderella," he muttered. "Hoping some prince would find them and come after you, ask you to marry him, or better yet, fund your restaurant?" That wasn't quite how the story went, but it was something like that. He wasn't a complete stranger to fairy tales. One of his nannies had read them to him when his father wasn't around. His father wanted him to read nothing but financial strategy and Horatio Alger books to inspire him, but the nanny had her own ideas.

Jack looked around the kitchen, and in his mind's eye, he saw Cinderella there at the stove, her hair curling in tendrils around her face, wonderful smells coming from the pots on the stove and from the oven.

If Hannah were here she'd rustle up something for him. But she'd called earlier to say that she'd broken her ankle and would have to stay off it for the rest of the week.

At the time he didn't know who to call to replace her. Now he knew.

Cinderella.

The next morning Jack called the number for Hostess Helpers but only got their answering machine. Frustrated, he tried several more times. When he still didn't get an answer, he started the seminar he was hosting at his house and then drove like a madman to their office on Union Street. He'd left a number of messages on their machine and had not received an answer. Was that any way to run a business?

He parked in a tow-away zone, got out, grabbed the glass slippers in one hand, slammed the door of his BMW and ran to the storefront office. The glass door that was inscribed with the slogan—"Hostess Helpers—For All Your Party Needs—We Make It Happen!"—was locked. It was nine-thirty, for God's sake. He peered into the empty office and banged on the door. A moment later, a well-preserved woman of about fifty came to the door. It must be the same woman he'd talked to on the phone when he'd arranged the party, but if she'd been at his house last night, he hadn't seen her.

"Sorry, we're not open until ten," she said, her lips arranged in a forced smile over tobacco-stained teeth.

"I'm looking for Cinderella," he said, holding up her glass slippers.

"Hah," said the woman, opening the door and reaching for the shoes. "I'll give them to her."

"No way," he said, stepping back. "I have to see her in person. About a job."

"Won't you come in?" the woman said after studying him for a long moment and obviously deciding he was worth her time. In seconds, her expression changed to one of exaggerated sweetness. "I have two other daughters who are available for parties or various affairs."

"Uh-uh," Jack said, picturing the two useless look-alikes from last night. "I want Cinderella. Just for a week. Can you tell me where to find her?"

The woman sighed loudly, then went to her desk and thumbed through an appointment book.

"Birthday party, 441 Lake Street. Outdoor, treasure hunt, trampoline. Ten to one. But I'm telling you, she's nothing by herself. She's part of our team. I'm afraid I can't…"

Jack didn't wait for her to finish her sentence. It took him only a few minutes to drive to 441 Lake Street. It was not yet ten o'clock, so there were no kids in sight. But the Hostess Helpers van was parked in the driveway, and behind a hedge, and he could hear the whir of a motor. He opened a gate and walked around the side of the house. There she was, pumping air into the inflatable trampoline with a long, snakelike hose and a motor.

The sound of the motor was so loud she didn't hear him arrive. She was wearing a pair of slim-fitting black pants and a yellow sweater that hugged her curves. Her blond hair made him think of sunshine even on this overcast San Francisco day. He took a moment to appreciate the view of those incredible legs and shapely breasts. This was the third version he'd seen of Cinderella. It took him a few minutes to adjust to the change.

Business, he told himself sternly. If she were some ordinary woman, and he wasn't in the middle of this project, he might ask Cinderella out. He'd impress her with a high-priced night on the town, take her back to his place as per the usual Jack Martin scenario, lure her into bed, then tactfully get rid of her before she got any ideas of permanence.

But this was no time for fooling around, especially not with her.

"Hey, Cinderella."

"What do you want?"

"Forgot your slippers."

"Keep them. They're too tight."

"I came to ask a favor."

A strange expression came over her face. He

couldn't tell if it was anger, surprise or disgust. Maybe a combination of all of those plus a hint of suppressed satisfaction. What had he done to deserve any of those?

"Look, what is it? You're not still mad because I turned you down are you? I thought I explained that."

"Yes, you did," she said briskly. "You explained it quite well."

Maybe it was the *way* he'd explained it. What was he supposed to say? People who want to borrow money to start a restaurant or any other small business have to be able to take the truth when it's presented to them or they're never going to make it.

"If I hurt your feelings I'm sorry."

"You think my feelings were hurt because you called me a nobody?"

Had he really said that? "I was speaking as an investor. Of course you're not a nobody. I didn't mean it the way it sounded. It's clear you're a somebody."

"Thanks." Her voice dripped sarcasm.

"Look, it's a dog-eat-dog world out there," he said, "in case you haven't noticed. I thought it was best you heard it from me. Because getting turned down happens to everyone, some more often than others."

"Even you?"

"Of course. Despite my diligence, I've put together deals that had fallen through. And I've pushed my investors into ventures that had failed despite their bright promise. Next time around they're more likely to turn me down. Oh, yes, it's happened to me."

But not this time. This time he'd put together a winning group of companies that were sure to succeed. All he had to do was to convince the big guns who were at that very moment a captive audience in his house, their mouths watering, waiting for a delicious lunch. He had to provide one, and not only lunch, but dinner and breakfast and so on for the rest of the week. On top of the gourmet food, he had to give them an enticing array of ventures to sink their teeth into. He had the show-and-tell lined up; that was no problem.

The problem was the food. And that problem could be solved by the vision standing in front of him, bursting with health and energy, and looking like an advertisement for some kind of party equipment. The only thing standing between him and success was this woman.

He didn't know her very well, but he knew what made people tick. Money. He was going to make her an offer she couldn't refuse. If she did, he had no backup. The look on her face, the determined way she held her shoulders reminded him of that day in his office. It threw a scare into him. Because it told him she *could* refuse if he didn't present it in the right way. Just as he'd refused her. He knew she hadn't forgotten that, and that it still rankled.

"You've caught me at a bad time," she said with a glance at her watch. "Although it's nice to see you again and all that, I have a party to put on, and I really don't have time to talk about what I felt or didn't feel. There will be twenty-five kids coming in fifteen minutes. And this pump is so slow. Meanwhile I have to unpack the party favors."

He looked around at the vast expanse of lawn and the balloons tied to the trees. "So all this is just for a kid's party?"

"If they have a home party. This is a rather modest one. No clowns, no ponies, no acrobats. Some parents take the kids someplace where they play arcade games and eat pizza. I prefer the at-home parties, more personal and tailored specially for the birthday child. And not just because it's my job to put on the parties."

"I see," he said. And he did. She came across as sincere and definitely not the type to fake it for the sake of her job.

"Don't you remember the parties you went to? I suppose your parties consisted of miniature train rides and a hired magician on your estate," she said.

"Hardly. First, we didn't live on an estate. I lived with my father in a condo on Russian Hill, no upkeep, no grass to cut, no room for trains or ponies. And no time for birthday parties. My father had no idea when my birthday is, still doesn't. He thought all that kid stuff was a waste of time."

She blinked. Was she shocked or did she feel sorry for him? He didn't want her pity.

"I never missed them, either," he added firmly. "Or the yard or the bicycle or the pony rides. What I did get was tennis camp, ski lessons and a math tutor. So don't feel sorry for me."

Then he took the pump handle out of her hand. His fingers brushed hers and he felt a charge of electricity shoot up his arm. Must have been a loose connection from the wire to the pump. "Let me do that," he said.

She hesitated only a moment, then she shrugged and went to her van. When she came back, he'd gotten the inflatable trampoline up on its four corners, pounded the stakes in with a sledgehammer and tied the whole thing down so it wouldn't blow away. Then he squeezed through the mesh opening and went in to see what it was like inside.

"What are you doing?" she called from outside the structure.

"Testing it. It says on the tag it holds up to 350 pounds. Come on in, unless…"

"I don't weigh three hundred pounds," she said as her head appeared through the small opening meant for kids. "If that's what you're wondering."

"Didn't think so," he said, letting his gaze slide up and down her slender body. In that outfit she was wearing that day in his office, he hadn't been able to tell what kind of body she had, except for the legs, of course. He had a better idea today, and who could blame him for taking a minute to appreciate it. She was an interesting package of talent and looks. He wondered idly if she had a boyfriend. After a long silence, he remembered they'd been talking about weighing three hundred pounds. "Neither do I," he said.

"Well, are you going to test it or not?"

"You first." Not only had there been no birthday parties, but he'd never been on a trampoline before.

She jumped up and down a few times, her breasts bouncing in a tantalizing way. So tantalizing he stood staring, forgetting for a moment why he was there. To shake himself out of his reverie, he started jumping, matching his jumps with hers. She smiled. He smiled back. She jumped higher. If he was anything, he was a competitor. So he jumped higher than her. Her hair was flying around her face. She fell on her butt. Her face was flushed and she looked like a kid. He let himself fall down next to her. She laughed out loud, a throaty, bubbling sound. He laughed, too. He couldn't help it. It was ridiculous. It was contagious. All those childhood years he'd been expected to behave, to act serious, like a little adult. Maybe he *had* missed out on something.

He didn't know how long they would have stayed there laughing like idiots, as if he had nothing more important to do than bounce on a trampoline with a stranger, if they hadn't heard the children's voices.

"Oh, my God," she muttered, smoothing her hair. "They're here." She started to crawl on hands and knees to the exit.

He grabbed her arm. "Wait, I haven't told you what I want."

She shook his hand off. "I have to go."

"It will only take a minute." Afraid she'd take off, he talked faster. "My housekeeper broke her ankle. I need you to fill in for her for a week. To cook, three meals a day for seven days."

"That's what you came here for? I can't. I'm busy. I'm sorry."

"I'll make it worth your while. I'll pay twice what you're getting here or elsewhere." That was a safe offer. How much could a kids' party planner make?

"No." She was at the exit now, her hair tumbling around her face, her sweater bunched up so he got a glimpse of a smooth firm stomach and round hips.

"What do you want? Name your price."

Her forehead puckered. She cocked her head and looked him in the eye. What was she thinking? He had no way of telling. Something was going through her mind; he could tell by her expression. This wasn't the first time he'd seen her thoughts reflected in her face, and he couldn't tear his eyes away. She wasn't beautiful. Her mouth was too wide, her nose a little too short, but those big expressive eyes had him mesmerized. He found himself holding his breath, wondering what she was going to say. She had to say yes. He'd do whatever it took to convince her.

"Not now," she said at last.

"What do you mean not now? When? I haven't got much time."

"Neither do I, and I can't talk now. I'll come to your house when I finish the party. But I warn you, my price is going to be high."

He shrugged and watched her crawl out without another word. He heard her greet the party guests with genuine enthusiasm. And they responded. It was obvious she had a rapport with kids. Maybe she even had a few of her own. For all he knew she was married. Cinderella married? She didn't say anything when they talked about Prince Charming.

She could be married. Why not? She was an attractive woman, very sexy when she bounced around and her hair came loose. Maybe she'd already found her prince and didn't feel like sharing that information with him. The thought made him feel strangely let down. Deflated, like the trampoline before he'd pumped it full of air. Married or not, she'd started the kids on a treasure hunt that gave him the opportunity to sneak out the gate without the hyperactive little demons giving him a second glance.

He got back to his house in time to check in on the seminar and order halfway decent take-out lunches. The group was in good spirits, having spent the morning being told about the opportunities to double their money in various high-tech fields like fiber optics. Jack wasn't worried about the presentations. He'd lined up an impressive list of guest speakers, who were all knowledgeable, stimulating and convincing.

But as he sat in on one of the lectures, he found his mind wandered. Where was Cinderella? Had he convinced her? She hadn't said yes, but she hadn't said no, either. Would she get there in time to make dinner? Hannah had planned all the menus and had all the ingredients on hand. All the woman had to do was follow the instructions. But if she didn't come... He didn't know what he'd do. It was too late to call another caterer. Restless, he ducked out of the meeting and walked outside to pace up and down on the sidewalk.

When he saw her van approach, his heart rate accelerated. She'd do it. She had to do it. He motioned for her to park in his driveway and he watched her step down gracefully. She was wearing khakis and a loose gray sweatshirt. He wondered what she'd look like in a backless black dress with that blond hair down on her bare shoulders. Where had that thought come from? The only thing he should be thinking was how she looked in an apron. She wasn't the type for black dresses, anyway, so he'd never know. If he got what he wanted, she'd be his cook for a week and that was it.

He made it a rule to never date anyone who worked for him. He'd been tempted. There'd been some hot women at the firm, but his father was right about not dipping his pen in company ink, and he hadn't regretted it. Why take chances, when there's a whole world of available women out there? Sophisticated ladies who understood that *forever after,* or even *tomorrow* or *next week* were not words in Jack's vocabulary.

He watched Cinderella walk toward him, her eyes locked with his, her step measured, and he couldn't tell from her expression what her answer would be. It had to be yes. Who wouldn't want to make more money? Unless it was attached to some hardship. This job wasn't. Unless she considered working for him a hardship. How could that be?

"Well?" he said, out of time and out of patience. He didn't have time to be charming, to beat around the bush and make small talk. "What's your price?"

"I want you to fund my restaurant."

"I can't do that. It's against company policy. My partners would think I'd lost my mind." Not to mention his father.

"Fine." She turned on her heel and started back to the van.

"Wait a minute. I'll triple your normal rate."

She glanced at him over her shoulder. "I don't care about the salary. Get someone else."

"I don't want someone else. I want you."

Her eyes narrowed. "Too bad."

He grabbed her arm for the second time that day.

"Wait a minute. You know I'm desperate. You're taking advantage of me. You're not playing fair."

"Fair? This is business. You're a businessman. It's a dog-eat-dog world out there. You told me to name my price. I did."

"You're talking about hundreds of thousands. Even if I wanted to…"

"Which you don't."

"Even if I wanted to, I couldn't fund a restaurant. I have to justify my investments."

"I understand," she said, pulling away.

"All right," he said, feeling the heat and the pressure, seeing his whole week go down the drain unless he acted fast. "I'll make you a deal. If this week goes the way I think it will, and I get the results the firm wants, I'll fund your little restaurant with my own money. But make no mistake. This is not charity. You'll have to show a profit in six months or I pull the plug."

"And if your whole thing falls through this week, despite the food I make?"

He shook his head. "Then we're both out of luck. You, presumably, will still have your kiddie party gig, but I may not be so lucky. I'd take a big loss. My reputation would be in tatters. I could lose my job and my house…" He gestured toward the imposing façade of the house behind him.

"Oh," she said, glancing back at the house with a worried frown.

"Don't worry," he said. It bothered him more than it should, seeing those etched lines on her forehead, so much that he reached out to smooth them, though he knew he shouldn't touch her. "I won't be out on the street. I always land on my feet."

Ellie wasn't worried about his living on the street. She was worried about the way he made her feel when his thumb smoothed her sensitive skin. Get hold of yourself, she warned. He didn't mean anything by it. This is business.

"Does that change your opinion about me?"

"I don't know you well enough to have an opinion about you," she said. That was a lie. Of course she'd formed an opinion of him the first time she'd seen him—money-grubbing, hard-hearted, cold and mean. Then who was the guy who was bouncing up and down on the trampoline with her this morning? The guy who'd never had a birthday party and acted like he didn't care but really did. He had to care, unless he was made of stone. That guy was someone else, someone she didn't expect to see again. He was trying to charm her. Had he succeeded? No way. Well, maybe just a little. Just for a minute.

He shot her a half smile that said, "Oh, yes, you

do have an opinion of me. Everyone does." He was perceptive, that was for sure. He had to be to be in the business of making people part with their money.

"So, Cinderella, don't go feeling sorry for me, even if everything crashes. I've stashed away something for a rainy day." He looked at the sky as if he wondered if this might be the day, then his gaze latched on to hers. "What do you say, Cinderella, are you a gambling girl?"

The question went unanswered when his phone rang. Now when he was distracted was her chance to walk away. If she really was serious, she'd do it. She turned. He hung up, grabbed her arm and turned her to face him.

"The answer is no. I don't gamble, not with money, anyway," she said.

"Come on, Cinderella. Take a chance. What have you got to lose, anyway?"

He was right; she'd always have Hostess Helpers, but how dull that seemed compared to taking charge of a kitchen, any kitchen, and making decisions on her own. Even if she was just doing a super catering job for a bunch of high rollers for a week. And if it failed and she didn't get her funding and she didn't work for her stepmother anymore? Then she'd be applying for sous-chef jobs at restaurants that paid minimum wage. It was a depressing thought. But at least she would have tried for her dream instead of living in her family's shadow.

"Okay," she said. "When do I start? And by the way, my name is Ellie."

He grinned. His eyes lit up. Her heart skipped a beat. She warned herself not to get taken in by a grin or smooth talk or a random touch of the hand. Because those were the tricks of the trade for a man who always got what he wanted. This guy was a professional charmer. Schmoozing money out of rich people and work out of poor people like her. She had to get everything in writing.

He must have read her mind. "Let's go into the house and we'll draw up a contract," he said. They walked past his living room, which was set up with chairs filled with well-dressed people listening to a speaker who was showing pictures on a screen of a "new product guaranteed to change your life forever." In his office—the kind of office she knew he'd have, filled with leather-bound books and big, comfortable chairs—he wrote up a contract on his large polished walnut desk, and they both signed it.

Ellie knew she ought to read the fine print, but for some crazy reason she trusted him, and besides, she wasn't a fine-print kind of girl. She was someone with vision, who looked at the big picture, and this big picture was of her very own restaurant. They shook hands, and he held hers a few seconds longer than necessary. Long enough for her heart to thump against her ribs. It was fear of the unknown, fear of failing, fear of falling. His hand was warm and solid. Hers was small and cold.

"Well, Cinderella, we've got a deal," he drawled.

Calm down, she told herself. If he could be that casual, so could she. She was working for him. He was paying her. Any feelings she had about him as a man were totally out of place. If she couldn't control her physical reactions to him, she ought to tear up the contract and walk away. Could people tear up contracts? They did it in the movies.

She admitted he was an attractive man and she was a vulnerable woman. When you got right down to it, he was risking more than she was.

"To set the record straight, I'm not Cinderella," she said. "Not anymore. I work for a living, sure, but I'm nobody's scullery maid. And I certainly never had a fairy godmother."

"Did you need one?"

"No, of course not. I had two parents. For a while, anyway. When it counted. After that, well, I could have used a little magic in my life from time to time," she said lightly, trying not to think of the loss of her mother and the arrival of Gwen and her stepsisters. She never understood how her father could have remarried within the year. And to Gwen of all people.

It made her aware of the difference between the sexes. How could her father have forgotten so soon? It seemed to her then and even now that his marriage to Gwen was a betrayal. He'd loved her mother. They hadn't had a perfect marriage. Who does? But he was faithful and so was she. They'd made a happy home for her. Sure, her father was lonely after her mother died. So was she. But why Gwen and why so soon? His precipitous second marriage and the arrival of her stepmother and sisters created a wedge between her and her father that was never closed.

"I don't believe in magic," he said flatly.

"Not even when you were a kid?"

"I was never a kid."

"That's right, no backyard, no birthday parties. You've probably never even been to the circus."

"The circus? Why would I want to go to the circus?" His forehead creased in a puzzled frown.

"I don't know. To see the clowns, acrobats and elephants and the high-wire acts, maybe. And stuff yourself with popcorn, peanuts and cotton candy. At least, that's why I went."

"Sounds like you've got some happy memories."

She nodded. "I was an only child. They doted on me. Bedtime stories, toys, books, the circus, until…" No use reliving the past. Before he could say anything, she changed the subject. "So your father taught you that kid stuff was a waste of time. Was your jumping on the trampoline today a case of arrested development?"

"Must have been," he said with a smile. He probably wished she'd forget about that breach of behavior, but she hadn't. It made him seem almost human. His phone rang. He took it out of his pocket, studied the number on the caller ID, then told whoever was calling, "Can't talk now. Call you later."

"Now, if you'll excuse me," he said to Ellie, "I'll go join the sharks. If you need anything, Hannah left her number pinned to the refrigerator. You can call her."

Standing in the middle of the big empty kitchen, Ellie almost missed her stepmother and sisters with their complaining and snide comments. It was too quiet, too clean and too empty in there, and the expectations were too huge. She stood for a long moment with her arms wrapped around her waist. She was scared. Not that she couldn't do the job. She'd dazzle those venture guys with her crème brûlée, her seared halibut and her mango cheesecake.

It was working for Jack Martin that frightened her. Someone whose heart was made of stone. Whose eyes reflected dollar bills. Not one-dollar bills, thousand-dollar bills. Her first impressions were never wrong. Sure he'd helped her out today. Sure he'd jumped up and down on a trampoline with her and laughed like an idiot. And he'd confided in her about his childhood. And then promptly wanted to forget he'd ever done any of those things. She understood that part. She could kick herself for talking about her own past. The circus and all that. And sure he'd offered her a chance to get her own restaurant. If things went according to his plan.

But he was using her. He was a cynical gambler and a businessman out to make money for himself. He didn't mind sharing it, and that was a good thing. But after this week, she was on her own. If all went well, she'd get her funding and then she had to put up or shut up. It was a scary proposition, but one she'd hoped and prayed for.

She wondered how much she'd see of Jack. Hadn't she signed what he called a "boiler plate" venture capital agreement that he'd have the right not only to pull the plug on her if she didn't show a profit in six months, but also to monitor his investment—which meant her? Which meant that he would be her board of directors, with the right to inspect her books and watch her expenditures and generally lean over her shoulder.

She couldn't worry about that now. After all, what were the chances that things would all fall into place so that in one week she could start planning her restaurant? It was too good to be true.

One minute her hopes skyrocketed with dreams of that little bistro on the bay she'd envisioned with a view of fishing boats out the window where ordinary people felt comfortable coming for fabulous, earthy food—cumin-crusted lamb chops, chicken sauté with pineapple salsa and eggplant manicotti. She'd

hire some really good people to work with her, serv-
ers and sous-chefs who understood the food. She'd
feed them and they'd be like family, working together for a common goal.

The next minute she saw the whole thing falling
through and having to beg Gwen to take her back. In
any case, she was closer right now than she'd ever
been to having her dream come true. And it was all
because of Jack Martin. She told herself to calm
down and concentrate on dinner. If she didn't, if the
group wasn't blown away by what she created, she'd
be sealing his doom as well as her own.

Chapter Three

"I'm going to be busy this week," Ellie told Gwen as she cradled the kitchen phone against her ear.

"I know you are. You have jobs all week long," Gwen said tartly. "Cocktail party tonight, ladies' lunch tomorrow, birthday party…"

"No, I mean I've been hired by the guy we worked for last night, Jack Martin. His housekeeper got sick and I'm filling in for her. All week."

"So that's what he wanted," she muttered. "How much is he paying you?"

"I…uh…" Oh, Lord, she'd forgotten to ask him. That's what kind of businesswoman she was. "Twice as much as I've been making." That was what he'd said, hadn't he?

"Humph. Well, I suppose we'll have to manage without you. Of course you'll put half of what he gives you back into the business."

"Your business?" Ellie asked incredulously.

"*Our* business. The family business."

Ellie couldn't believe Gwen's attitude. She'd worked hard for the family and what had she gotten out of it? Certainly no thanks. Even though she'd done everything they'd ever asked. She'd put up with their orders and their short tempers and their self-centeredness. But this time Gwen had gone too far and Ellie'd had enough.

Ellie took a deep breath. "Look, Gwen, this is *my job*. He hired *me*. I'm the one who's going to do the work. It's just for a week. But what I earn this week I'm going to keep. All of it. Every penny. Do you hear?"

She imagined Gwen's mouth falling open. Her being too shocked to reply. Ellie talking back? Ellie refusing to take orders? She couldn't believe it. Ellie felt a rush of satisfaction.

"Talk to you later," Ellie said.

"Wait a minute. We need the van. Where is it?"

"Parked in front of his house."

"I'll have May come and pick it up."

"But…" How would she get home? Never mind. No time to worry about that now.

Ellie found that Jack's housekeeper had made a menu for the whole week, with recipes typed out and bound in a loose-leaf notebook, and had all the ingredients labeled. Some were in the huge freezer, some in the walk-in pantry. Some items, like the fish for the soup tonight, would be delivered. It was a dream come true. Ellie was chopping onions when the phone rang. She hesitated. Would Jack answer or should she? What did a housekeeper do exactly, besides cook? Clean? Take messages?

She soon found out because it was Hannah on the phone.

"I feel just terrible about this," Hannah said, when Ellie introduced herself. "Jack called and told me what a trooper you are, coming in at the last minute. I owe you, my dear, for giving up whatever you were doing.

"Jack tells me you're quite a cook. Feel free to change any recipes you want. They're not written in stone, you know. And Jack won't mind."

"He won't?"

Hannah chuckled. "I know how he comes across, all full of himself and demanding, but he'll respect you for standing up to him. You've probably seen his picture in the society column and read the comments, 'Jack Martin, playboy, with his latest girlfriend,' but that's not the Jack I know. That's not the *real* Jack. Sure, he looks like a wolf, even acts like one sometimes, but he's really a lamb underneath. Once you get to know him."

Which would never happen, Ellie thought. "I'm afraid I won't have time to get to know him. I'll only be here a week."

"True, true. I'll be back by then. Maybe not as good as new, but at least I'll be hobbling around. I hope your family won't miss you too much this week."

"As a matter of fact…"

"Your husband will be lost without you, is that what you mean?" Hannah asked.

"No, I'm not married, but I have a stepmother and two stepsisters who I work with."

"And I hear your name is Cinderella," Hannah said. "Very interesting."

"That was just for a children's party. I'm really just plain Ellie."

"Well, Ellie, my sister is here with a pot of soup she made. Can't cook worth a darn, but her heart's in the right place. Be right with you, Clara. Oh, yes, the neighbor girls I hired ought to show up at seven to serve. They know what to do. I trained them myself. You'll be busy enough cooking. If they give you any trouble, you let me know. And don't believe those rumors about our Jack. He's a sweetheart. Just needs a good… Never mind. Now, Ellie, you call me anytime, you hear?"

Feeling cheered by the woman's comments, she was also puzzled by her assessment of Jack's character. But then, Jack probably paid Hannah plenty for her services, which included praising her boss. Ellie went back to chopping onions and sautéing veal and scallops for the main course. By the time the fish man came to the back door, she had the soup base made and was ready to put it all together. A few minutes before seven o'clock, two teenage girls came to the back door, dressed in matching black dresses.

"We're here to serve," they explained. "I'm Stephani and she's Lauren. Too bad about Mrs. Armstrong, but she said you're just as good, and you're the boss." They peeked into the pots and sniffed appreciatively. "Smells good," they said.

"Are you Jack's new girlfriend?" Stephani asked.

"Oh, no, no," Ellie said with a little more emphasis than was absolutely necessary. "Substitute cook, that's it. I'm a chef, a *professional* chef. I just met him yesterday."

"We were wondering. That is my mom was wondering because the women in the neighborhood have a pool going. They guess how long his latest girlfriend will last. Sometimes it's a week, sometimes a month."

Ellie looked at her watch. "Well, girls, I guess we'd better get going."

They nodded, tied aprons around their waists and were soon filling water glasses at the long dinner table in the dining room and folding napkins in a cheerful efficient manner her stepsisters would do well to emulate. If they cared enough, which they didn't.

Jack poked his head into the kitchen. "Ready?"

She wiped her palms on her apron and nodded. She shouldn't be nervous. Everything had been planned. She'd tasted and basted and added a few things to the recipes. She had help. Real help, not stepsister help. She had confidence. But her heart was hammering. She stood at the entrance to the dining room and pressed her ear against the door. She heard loud voices and laughter. She heard Jack's voice proposing a toast and glasses clink together. Then she went back to the kitchen.

Salad was tossed. Rolls were heated. Soup was ladled. Plates were filled, bowls were passed. Dessert was consumed. Coffee was made and drunk.

Three hours later the dinner was over. The voices faded as the group adjourned to the living room. The girls started to wash the pots and pans and load the dishwasher.

"Don't you have homework?" she asked them.

They nodded in unison.

"Go home. I can do this."

"Sure?"

"Yes."

"Really? We're supposed to—"

"I know. You're supposed to do the pots and pans, but I remember high school. Yes, it was about a hundred years ago, but I still remember staying up late to do my homework and getting up early for my first class."

"Thank you," they chorused, took off their aprons and headed for the door. "We just live across the street. We'll be back tomorrow."

"Thanks," Ellie said as they closed the door behind them. She poured herself a cup of coffee heavily laced with cream, and sank into the chair in the corner.

That's where Jack found her a few minutes later. He gave her a thumbs-up.

"Was it all right?" she asked, still in a daze. Still unable to stand and face the pots and pans.

"All right? It was great! If they don't come around, it won't be your fault. Some of the women asked for your recipes, or rather Hannah's recipes. How're you holding up? You look beat."

She managed to force a tired smile.

He looked around the kitchen. "Where are the girls?"

"I sent them home. They had homework. When I was their age…" She blinked back a tear before he could see it.

"Go on."

"Nothing."

"When you were their age you were out every night or on the phone with your friends, am I right?"

"My mom died when I was eleven. I was suddenly in charge of the house until my dad remarried."

"So those were the bad times."

"They weren't that bad until Gwen and the girls moved in," she said.

"So you could stop cooking and go back to being a kid."

"Not exactly. I didn't stop cooking, I just had to cook what she wanted me to." The memories came flooding back. The feelings of being dictated to, left out, forgotten by her father and unloved. She shook her head and pressed her lips together to keep from blurting something she'd regret. Jack was not interested in her past. She'd already said far too much. This was a business relationship and that was all. Jack didn't say anything. He just looked away, took off his suit coat and rolled up his sleeves. She'd embarrassed him, and herself, too, by blabbing on and on. It was just because she was tired.

"I'd better give you a hand."

"Don't you have homework, too?" she asked, rising slowly from her chair.

"I do have work. I have to crunch some numbers before tomorrow, but I'm a night owl and I have plenty of time to do it. The gang has gone to North Beach to sample our night life, but I pleaded other commitments. They'll be back tomorrow morning. Can I say the same for you?" His tone was light, but there was a hint of anxiety in his gaze. Did he really think she'd walk out on him after only one night? She was not a quitter.

"Of course. We have a deal." She filled the sink with hot water and added a splash of liquid detergent.

He patted her on the shoulder. His way of being friendly, of protecting his investment, no doubt. "Just checking," he said.

She wasn't surprised when his cell phone rang, and he carried on a conversation while stacking pots with one hand.

"Don't you ever turn your phone off?" she asked when he hung up.

"Might miss something. Especially this week. There's so much on the line. Every call is important."

"So how is it going?" she asked, her hands submerged in soapy water.

"So far, so good." He picked up a towel and dried one of the roasting pans. "But it doesn't mean anything. I've put on these things before and got nothing, zilch, nada."

"You still have your job."

"Yeah, but you never know. You're only as good as your latest investment."

"You seem to be doing all right. Nice house."

"With a nice mortgage."

"Still…"

"I can't complain."

"Your parents must be proud of you."

"I wouldn't say proud. My dad expects a lot from me, always has. My mom…that's another story."

She didn't say anything and neither did he. This was not the time for confidences, at least on his side. She only wished she'd kept her mouth shut. She'd already heard enough about his father. And she didn't need to hear about his mother. She was just making conversation.

She handed him a large china soup tureen to dry. His fingers brushed hers. She felt a charge of electricity race up her arm. Had he felt it, too? A glance in his direction told her nothing. He didn't blink, didn't flinch. It was her, only her. And it was late. He was helping her, and she was grateful, but she was also tired and vulnerable. That's all it was.

She washed the last pot, and he dried it.

"Not to put any undue pressure on you, but I promised eggs Benedict for breakfast," he said.

"That's no problem. I do a mean hollandaise sauce."

"I can't imagine you doing a mean anything, Cinderella." He reached around her waist and untied her apron. His eyes gleamed and his face was so close to hers she was afraid to meet his gaze, afraid of what she might see. Afraid of what he might see. Her heart pounded.

The kitchen door burst open. "Jack?"

Ellie stumbled backward.

"Sorry to butt in."

"That's okay, Rick." Jack's voice sounded tight.

The man raised his eyebrows. "So this is your housekeeper? I thought she was older."

"She is. I mean this isn't her. This is my...just a temp."

You're just a temp, Ellie told herself. No more, no less. And don't you forget it.

"And does your temp need a ride home? Looks like she's ready to collapse. That was some dinner, lady."

"Thank you." Ellie leaned back against the counter, trying to get her breath back, trying to keep her knees from buckling.

"I'm taking her home," Jack said firmly.

"That's not necessary," she said. "I can call a cab."

"I'll meet you out in front," Jack said. The tone of his voice was the one he doubtlessly used on businesses who dared try to do things their way and not his. It was a small thing, so she did what he said and met him out in front.

"Where's your van?" he asked, looking up and down the street.

"May came to pick it up. They need it this week. It's okay, I can manage."

"You live with them?" he asked as he drove through the streets, the engine of his late-model BMW purring like a cat, all leather interior with heated leather seats and soft music coming from the speakers.

"I have my own apartment in Noe Valley. Working and living with them would be a little much. Turn right at the next light. Third house on the right."

He opened the door for her. "I'll come by and get you in the morning. Is eight too early?"

"I can take the bus."

"And if it breaks down or it doesn't come on time? How am I supposed to make hollandaise sauce? I'll be here at eight."

"Better make that seven."

"Deal."

Jack watched her walk up the steps to the flat in the Victorian house. She didn't turn to wave or say good-night. But he stood there on the sidewalk, watching while lights went on on the third floor. A shadow passed in front of the window. Was it Ellie or someone else? She hadn't said she lived alone. She might have a boyfriend waiting for her up there. She'd never really said if she was married or not. He'd just assumed... The thought of some man waiting for her made his jaw tighten. Why should he care? Her private life was her own.

He wondered what he'd gotten himself into. He wished he hadn't promised he'd invest his own money in her restaurant. He couldn't afford to get involved in anyone's life, especially not someone he was investing in. Damn. It was too late to back out now. If he got the funds he needed, then he'd owe it to her and he'd have to go through with it.

There was something about her that worried him. More accurately, there was something about the effect she had on him that worried him more. She wasn't his type. Not at all. But when he looked in those big brown eyes, he forgot about his mission, forgot about the past, forgot about his future and only thought about her. Tonight he'd almost kissed her in the kitchen. He might have, if they hadn't been interrupted. What was wrong with him? Was he working too hard? Worrying about the project? Was that an excuse for losing his cool and contemplating kissing the kitchen help?

Even now he was inexplicably angry for the interruption in the kitchen when he should be grateful. Tomorrow he'd be careful. No more late-night sessions in the kitchen or anywhere else. Just get through the week. And if all went well, and he succeeded, he'd give her the money and leave her to start her restaurant. He wouldn't lean over her shoulder. He wouldn't be her board of directors. He'd take a backseat. He'd get on with his life. He'd call other women and he'd go out and socialize. Women who understood. Women who didn't look at him the way she did. Women who didn't encourage him to act like the kid he never was.

But was that her fault or his that he had jumped around on a trampoline? Hadn't he really wanted to show her he wasn't made of stone? Hadn't he wanted to make her smile, even make her laugh? And standing there on the sidewalk, the collar of his jacket up against the wind, staring up at the third floor, trying to make out silhouettes behind the window, didn't he want to hear her laugh again?

A lot of questions, but no answers. He turned away from her house, drove himself home and went straight to his office. There he tried to concentrate on figures, but all he could see was her figure. All he could think of was being interrupted by Rick. If Rick hadn't come into the kitchen, Jack might have violated all of his own rules and kissed his temporary cook. Good thing he hadn't. She might have been offended. Or she might have kissed him back.

He didn't know which was worse. Either way it would have added a complication to their already complicated relationship. He gave up and went to bed, but not to sleep.

Before Jack knew it, it was dawn, and he was up and on his way back to Ellie's house to pick her up. His cell phone rang while he was at the corner of Pacific and Divisadero.

"Jack, how is everything going?" Hannah asked.

"Fine, how are you?"

"Oh, you know. It's hard to have to depend on others. I want to know how my replacement is doing."

"Fine," Jack said carefully.

"That's good to hear," she said. "I talked to her

yesterday, and she sounds like a lovely girl. What does she look like?"

"Tall, blond hair, brown eyes, slim, why?"

"No reason. I just wondered. Anything wrong with her?"

"Only that she's not you. Is that what this is about? You're afraid she'll replace you? Never. She has no desire to work for me. She wants to start her own restaurant."

"She's not married, you know."

No, he didn't know and he wasn't going to ask. "Right," he said. Was that a silent sound of relief inside his head? Of course not.

"Do you like her?"

"Of course I like her. Would I have asked her to help out if I didn't like her? She's nice and she's a good cook. Not as good as you, of course, but not bad."

"There are other things, Jack, besides cooking."

"I don't know what you mean. You wouldn't be matchmaking, would you, Hannah?" Hannah made no secret of her disapproval of Jack's lifestyle when it came to women—or work for that matter. She maintained that he worked too hard and went out with the wrong kind of women. He avoided bringing women to the house for fear Hannah would give them the cold shoulder. It wasn't hard to see where she was going with this conversation.

"Matchmaking?" she sniffed. "Of course not.

Well, I'd better go. I'll call you later. Just to see how things are going."

"Do that. And take it easy. Everything's under control."

But he wasn't sure of that, especially when Ellie came down the steps of her house dressed in skinny jeans and a bulky green sweater that brought out flecks of green in her eyes he hadn't known were there.

"What is it?" she asked. "Why are you looking at me that way?"

"What way?" He tore his eyes away and opened the car door for her.

"Like I'm some rare specimen you've got under a microscope."

"Just wondering," he said casually. "If there is a Prince Charming."

"Maybe somewhere, but not in my life," she said.

"Not looking for one?"

"No."

"Playing the field?"

"Like you do? Hardly."

"What do you know about me?"

"Just what your cook, Hannah, told me."

"What did she do, warn you off?" He grinned at her as he swerved around a slow truck and sped up the hill toward Pacific Heights. "Never mind. You didn't need any warnings. You'd already made up your mind about me."

"That wasn't hard," Ellie said. "But, actually, Hannah spoke highly of you," Ellie said, looking straight ahead.

"She has to. She works for me. You didn't listen to her, did you? Even if she was sincere, that's just one woman's opinion. Most people think I'm a hard-hearted bastard. Oh, by the way, you get tonight off. Part of the San Francisco experience I want them to enjoy is the symphony gala. It just happened to be this week, so I got tickets for the whole group. Expensive, but I think it will pay off."

She nodded but she didn't say anything. She certainly didn't disagree with his description of himself as hard-hearted, probably because of that initial meeting. Since then he didn't *think* he'd acted like a jerk. But that was open to interpretation. It really didn't matter what she thought as long as she did her job. She didn't have to like him or approve of his lifestyle. He didn't care one way or another.

He'd get out his little black book and round up a date for tonight. One that would turn heads with her perfectly coiffed hair; expensive, high-fashion dress and outrageous jewelry. Just the kind of woman he liked to be seen with. Not that he ever had much to say to any of them, but did that really matter? Not tonight it didn't. It was all about appearances.

Chapter Four

Ellie was already exhausted, and the day wasn't even half over. After she'd finished serving eggs Benedict to the group along with fresh-squeezed orange juice, she'd loaded the two dishwashers and started lunch preparations. A delivery truck brought boxes of fresh produce and she sniffed a box of deep-red, perfectly ripe strawberries appreciatively. The deliveryman asked for a check, and Ellie went to look for Jack. She tiptoed past the main room where the seminar was in progress, looked in but didn't see him. She paused outside his office and knocked softly.

"Yes, what?" he said brusquely.

She opened the door. Jack was sitting behind his

desk, glowering at his feet, which were propped up on his desk.

"I need a check for the green grocer. Fifty-three dollars."

He scribbled his name and the amount on a check and slid it across the desk. "What's for lunch?"

"Hearts of romaine with a Point Reyes blue cheese dressing and pasta pomodoro. Crème brûlée with fresh strawberries for dessert. Is that all right?"

"Of course it's all right." He twisted his pen between his thumb and fingers. "What are you doing tonight?"

"I don't know. You just told me I had the night off. I haven't had time to make plans."

"But you're going to, right?"

Really, the man was unbelievable. What right did he have to delve into her personal life? She wasn't even his employee. She was just a temp. "Is this the way you treat Hannah?"

"You mean with generosity by giving her the night off?"

"I mean by prying into her affairs."

He acted like she hadn't spoken. "I have an extra ticket for the symphony gala, fifth-row-center seats with dinner beforehand. All of the women I'd normally ask are busy and I thought you might want to—"

"I'm busy," she said. Did he actually think she'd fill in at the last minute and hobnob with this crowd who might have seen her scrubbing pots and pans? She could just imagine the curious looks, the hidden smiles, the speculation.

Who's that?

What's she doing here?

She's not even dressed right.

No, it was out of the question.

"But you just said you hadn't made plans," he said.

She waved the check in her hand. "I just did. I have a date with a good book. Now if you'll excuse me, I can't keep the delivery boy waiting."

To her dismay, Jack followed her down the hall to the kitchen, and watched the boy take his check and walk out the back door. Then he leaned against the door as if he had nothing better to do, his arms crossed over his waist, his hair looking as if he'd been raking it. When he wasn't looking smooth and suave in coat and tie, he looked disarmingly engaging. Either way he was a force to be reckoned with, and she'd be a fool to let down her guard. He could do some serious damage to her self-control.

"Aren't you curious about the cuisine at the gala? After all, the caterer is Suzanne Pelletier, wouldn't she be one of your competitors?"

Was she curious? Yes. Would she say so? No way. "Suzanne Pelletier my competitor? I don't think so. She's so out of my league. All I want is to open a neighborhood bistro, which you'd know if you'd listened to me. As you so kindly pointed out to me, I'm no celebrity chef. Nor do I want to be."

"Still, you might want to check out the food. Her reputation may be all hype. It's got to be hard to put on a gala spread for two hundred in the foyer of the opera house. You'd better come along and see how she does it."

"Is that an order?"

"Of course not. I don't order my employees around. I only suggest. And I suggest you be ready at six o'clock. I'll pick you up then." Without waiting for an answer, he strode out of the room.

She stood there with her mouth open in disbelief. She didn't have time to argue with Jack. She had to make lunch. She put Jack and his gala symphony out of her mind. Or she tried to. He had a way of coming between her and the salad dressing, between her and the propane torch she used on the crème brûlée. Not physically, of course, it was just the sound of his voice in her ear, the vision of his face, the determined set to his jaw that threatened her composure just when she needed it. He was determined? Well she was, too. And she was not going to be bullied into going out on the town with his crowd when she could curl up with a good book.

She was wiping down the counters with a sponge after lunch when the phone rang. It was Hannah, Jack's housekeeper.

"How are you feeling?" Ellie asked, perching on a stool.

"I'm fine as long as I keep off my foot," she said. "Jack tells me he invited you to the gala tonight."

Ellie sighed. Had he called everyone to tell them what he'd done and what she'd said? "Did he tell you I turned him down?" And did he tell you he doesn't take no for an answer?

"Well, he said you weren't very enthusiastic. He's very disappointed. He needs a date."

"That shouldn't be a problem. I'm sure he has a large selection of women to choose from. Why me? Why not them?" she asked Hannah.

"I have to confess it was my idea that he ask you. Good food, good music. I thought you might enjoy it. I'd go in a minute. If I could walk, that is."

Ellie didn't know what to say. She didn't want Hannah to think she was ungrateful. "It's not that I'm not grateful to you. I really appreciate the offer, but…uh, I wouldn't have anything to wear to a gala affair. I've seen the pictures in the society column—it's formal." There, that ought to do it.

"Formal? Nothing to wear? I can take care of that. I told you I owed you for filling in for me this week. I'm looking for a way to repay you. I told you Clara can't cook, but on the other hand, she's a crackerjack seamstress. Mother taught one of us to cook and the other to sew. Clara can't cook worth a darn and I can't even sew a button on. She's here to take care of me, but that's a boring job. She needs a challenge. I need some fresh company. And you need a fairy god-mother or two. So hustle on over here and we'll put something together for you."

"Well, that's very kind, but…"

"Not kind at all. Just practical and self-serving. How much time can I sit around and watch daytime TV? I miss Jack and I miss my job. Jack's life is al-ways more interesting than a soap opera, and truth-fully I need a distraction. I'm just being selfish, but somehow maybe I can pay you back for what you're doing for me this week. I'm bored. So is Clara. Yes, you are, don't deny it. She doesn't have any daugh-ters or granddaughters to sew for. So you'd be doing us a favor. Now that lunch is over, and a delicious one it was, I'm sure, how soon can you be here?"

What could Ellie say to that without sounding like a churlish, unappreciative girl? So she agreed to walk the five blocks to Hannah's apartment, in an hour.

Hannah's apartment was on the fifth floor of a stately old stone building on the corner. Clara let Ellie in and led her down a long, narrow hall to the living room, which was small with a high ceiling and a huge bay window with a view of the Golden Gate Bridge. Ellie imagined Hannah would be small and round with apple cheeks, but even when seated on a leather couch with her leg propped on a foot-stool, Ellie could see she was tall and thin with short gray hair. There was a sewing machine in the middle of the room and a large wicker basket with reams of fabric spilling over the sides on the table.

"Come in, come in," Hannah called, though Ellie was already in. "You must be Ellie. Turn around dear. See, Clara, I told you she'd be the chiffon type." She reached for a bolt of pale, soft fabric from the basket. "And tall enough to carry it off." Hannah beamed at Ellie as if she'd planned the whole thing. Maybe she had. Still, how could anyone make a dress in one afternoon?

"Look at that hair," Hannah continued. "A few curls and it will be perfect with chiffon and ruffles."

"I really don't think…it's not that I'm not grateful, but I don't think I'm the type." Not only was she not the ruffles and curls type, she was not the type for hobnobbing with high society.

"Not the type? Of course you are," Hannah said.

"Wait." Clara stood in the middle of the room, her hands on her hips. She looked younger than her invalid sister, but with the same angular features and straight, no-nonsense gray hair. "Hannah, drop the chiffon, you're being your usual overbearing bossy self. Why not ask Ellie what type she is and what kind of dress she'd like."

Ellie had to smile at the good-natured banter between the sisters. That's the way it should be, she thought. But I got stuck with April and May.

Ellie didn't know what to say about the dress. She knew what she would like, but how could she ask a total stranger to make her a black slinky dress that clung to her body?

"Hannah tells me you're Cinderella," Clara said, "so let's just say for the sake of argument, that we really are your fairy godmothers, and you can have whatever dress you want. Here." Clara handed her a fashion magazine, and indicated Ellie should sit next to her sister on the couch.

It didn't take long for her to find the dress she wanted. It was long, with a slit up the back to the knee, with thin spaghetti straps. It was sleek, it was chic and it was simple. Ellie had never had a dress like that in her life. It was not something Cinderella would wear to a children's party. It was strictly an adult dress for an adult affair. The kind of affair Ellie read about but never went to.

Clara nodded when she saw the one Ellie was looking at. "Perfect," she said, "and I know just where to get the fabric." She turned to Hannah. "In your closet."

"What do you mean?" Hannah said, bracing her elbows so she could sit up straight.

"It's the dress you wore to Uncle Fred's funeral. I'm sure it's still there. You never get rid of anything."

"But I can't wear your dress," Ellie protested to Hannah, thinking black silk, high neckline and long sleeves.

"I was going to take it to the thrift store, really I was, but I never got around to it. I certainly don't plan to wear it again."

Clara chuckled. "Not without some major adjustments."

"See, I told you I shouldn't give it away." Hannah was beaming. "I knew she'd come through," she said to Ellie. "She's a magician. You'll see. She once made a prom dress for me in an afternoon. That was about a hundred years ago, but she hasn't lost her touch. Go get it."

Ellie's heart sank when she saw the dress. It was just as she'd feared—matronly with a high neck, long sleeves and a full skirt. Nothing like the one in the magazine. But it did have yards and yards of black material—a wonderful silky material.

Clara, ripped and tore and cut and pieced the fabric, then pinned and finally stitched. Ellie stripped down to her sports bra and cotton bikinis to try on each and every permutation while the two sisters argued and bickered about what should be done.

"Tighter!"

"Looser!"

"Longer."

"Shorter."

In between fittings Hannah told stories about Jack. Ellie listened attentively. It was clear the woman thought the world of him. As he did of her. They had a mutual admiration society going that Ellie was not a part of, nor did she want to be. Obviously, the man had a side to him she hadn't seen, or else he'd completely fooled his cook. Either way, it didn't matter to Ellie. Sure, she believed Jack could be a nice, normal guy, at least while drying dishes for her or jumping on a trampoline. But was that enough? Not for her. Not for the average female. Did Jack care? Obviously not.

At the end of the afternoon Clara sat down at her sewing machine to do the final stitching. And when she finally finished, she stood and held up the most spectacular dress, a simple, black, elegant number that looked amazingly like the one in the magazine. If Ellie hadn't believed in magic before, she did now.

When Ellie tried it on, it was hard to imagine who was more pleased with the results—Hannah, Clara or Ellie.

It fit the way no store-bought dress would ever fit, as if it were made for Ellie. And it was. Ellie stood facing the full-length mirror in the bedroom staring at her reflection. Who was that woman there and where was she going?

Feeling like the recipient of an extreme makeover, Ellie walked slowly back into the living room. Hannah clapped her hands gleefully, looking tired but pleased and proud of her sister. She demanded that to repay them, Ellie had to give them a blow-by-blow account of the evening. Then Clara drove her home with the dress in a plastic bag and with only a half hour to spare. Before driving away, she blew Ellie a kiss from the car. It seemed incredible that she'd only known these women for an afternoon. As Ellie fumbled with her key at the front door, the kindness of these two heretofore strangers brought a tear to her eye. She'd store up enough information tonight to make a good story to tell them tomorrow. Even if she had to make up the whole thing.

It was a good thing Ellie didn't have any more time to think about the evening, or she might have panicked. As it was, her sister April called just as she was winding her long, straight, blond hair around the curling iron, trying to coax it into shape.

"I thought you were working all week," April said petulantly.

If she thought Ellie was working, why did she call her at home, Ellie wondered.

"I am. I'm just changing clothes, then I have to go, uh, back to work." No way would she disclose her actual evening plans, though it really was a part of her work. But April, May and Gwen would misunderstand. They'd think it was a date. They'd be jealous. They'd be angry. They'd be resentful. They'd want to know what she was wearing.

"What's he like?" April asked.

"Who?" Ellie asked innocently.

"You know, your boss, that millionaire."

"Opinionated and self-assured, that's what he's like. He likes to give orders. But it's okay, it's only for a week. I have to go, April. Talk to you later."

Ellie smeared a light foundation on her face, wondering why April had called, anyway. Just checking up on her? It was a relief not to have to see them every day. Then she applied a little mascara, wriggled into the dress and a pair of strappy sandals May had handed down to her when she bought a new pair, and ran to the door when the bell rang.

Jack looked so serious in his tux and black tie and so heart-stoppingly good-looking, Ellie couldn't move or speak.

The same problem seemed to have struck him. He stopped in the doorway and stood there like a statue. It wasn't fair. So rich, so handsome and yet so unavailable. Who could compete with his business? He could probably have any woman he wanted, if he made the ultimate sacrifice and put them ahead of his work, but all he seemed to care about was money. On the other hand, maybe women saw through that handsome facade to the heart of stone within. He stood in the doorway for so long without speaking, she was afraid something terrible had happened.

"Anything wrong?" she asked, catching her breath at last, and waving him into the living room.

"Turn around."

She pivoted. There was something wrong with the dress. That's what it was. The black silk swooshed around her legs. Maybe it wasn't appropriate. Too tight. Too much skin showing. Too low in back. Too low in front. Or something. She had a sinking feeling in the pit of her stomach.

"Where'd you get the dress?" he asked at last, his voice sounding like he was choking.

"Hannah."

"This is her dress?"

Ellie laughed nervously. "It was, but her sister made it over for me. In one afternoon. It was magic. Forget I said that, you don't believe in magic."

"I might have to change my mind."

"I know there'll be a lot of women in designer dresses in attendance. I just hope I won't stand out."

"You'll stand out," he said with a certain edge in his voice that made her pulse quicken. She didn't know quite how to take that. All she could do was to tell herself not to get carried away.

Jack adroitly switched the subject; they went to his car, and he kept his eyes on the road and talked business all the way to the symphony. He talked about the seminar, the various enterprises he wanted to fund, and gave her a description of the money men he was hosting this week. She was relieved they were on an impersonal subject. He was her boss and she was his temporary cook in a fancy dress. She wasn't a date. She hoped she wouldn't stand out. She hoped no one would notice her or wonder who she was.

The domed symphony hall was near the Civic Center, across the street from the Greek Revival city hall that was illuminated and stood out in the night sky, a homage to the classic period. Jack gave his car to a valet, and he put his hand on her bare arm as they climbed the steps to the wide doors of the hall.

A frisson of excitement shimmied up her spine, caused by the highly charged atmosphere, the crowds of well-dressed symphony patrons, the smell of money and expensive perfume, her dress and Jack. After all, in that dress, with his hand on her arm, he made her feel like she belonged there. That she was just as attractive, just as well turned out, just as classy as everyone else. A brief glance around told her he was the best-looking man on the premises, and just for tonight he was her escort.

Let people think what they like. She knew this was all business. She knew she was not his type, not a woman who attended the symphony nor mixed with the rich and well connected. Her place was behind the scenes, peering out from behind the kitchen door, hearing praise for the food and taking satisfaction from that.

Just a glance around at the acres of designer dresses, glittering jewelry and off-season-in-the-Caribbean tanned skin told her she was in a different world. But after the way Jack looked at her, she had confidence that she didn't stand out. She felt the knot of anxiety in her stomach start to dissolve.

In the foyer there were tables set with faux birch trunks, green leaves and votive candles, all of which, Ellie gathered, added up to a "Silver Starlight" theme. There were women in glittery silver gowns, too, but Ellie was content in black, more than content. And if she was completely honest with herself, she had to admit that Jack's admiring glances that came her way helped a lot to boost her confidence.

"I have to warn you," Jack said as they walked across the marble floor. A waiter came by with a tray of champagne before he could finish his sentence.

Oh-oh. Here it comes. She knew what he was going to say. Don't tell anyone who you are. Don't tell anyone you're with me.

"My father will be here," he said, leaning down to whisper her ear. "He can be…difficult."

"In what way?" she asked. Jack's warm breath on her ear sent a shiver up her bare back.

"In every way. There he is now. Oh, hello, Dad. I want you to meet Ellie. Ellie, this is my dad, Spencer Martin."

Jack's father was almost as good-looking as Jack,

tall and tanned and fit looking. He made no secret of scrutinizing Ellie from head to toe and holding her hand after he shook it.

Then he gave Jack a quizzical look.

"I'm just his cook," Ellie blurted.

Jack's eyes widened in surprise. His lips twitched and his grip on her arm tightened.

"I'm filling in. Just temporarily," she added. She didn't know what had gotten into her. It must have been the atmosphere, so heavy, so rich, so unreal, so beyond her reach, that made her want to make a statement. Though she loved children's parties, this kind of party was not what she was used to.

"Good to see you, Dad," Jack lied. He'd hoped to avoid his father tonight. He didn't want his opinion or his advice. He didn't want a lecture about women. He didn't want to explain Ellie. Jack was not thinking well, if he was, he would have taken steps to avoid his father. In fact, Jack wasn't thinking at all. He didn't know what was wrong with him, but everything, the furnishings, the crowd all seemed in soft focus.

Everything but Ellie, his replacement cook. She stood out clearly. In that black dress, with her creamy skin and her blond hair, she was a knockout. There were other beautiful women in the room. At least he thought there were. But he didn't see them. He only saw her. He not only saw her, he saw things through her eyes, those big, brown expressive eyes. He'd never seen the symphony hall looking more spectacular, he'd never noticed the marble floors and the sculptures in the alcoves. Not only that, but there was something in the air, something that hadn't been there the last time he was here, a sense of excitement, a promise of things to come that he thought she felt, too.

It had something to do with the shock he'd gotten when she'd opened her front door. That must be the reason he felt the way he did. The shock of seeing her dressed up. The woman was a chameleon. First she was in a short skirt at his office, next she was Cinderella in that ridiculous costume and bare feet. Then she was the kid jumping up and down on the trampoline. And now this. He didn't know what to make of her. He didn't know what to expect from her. And when he'd banged his head against hers in his kitchen, maybe he really had suffered a minor concussion. He sure had some strange symptoms. He wondered if she had them, too.

Jack noticed his father was studying him, his father's narrowed gaze traveling from Jack to Ellie.

"Can I have a word alone with you, son?" Spencer asked.

Jack shrugged and asked Ellie if she would excuse him for a moment. She nodded. He and his father walked toward the bar.

"I don't want to pry into your private life, Jack," his father said, stopping by the wall.

"Then don't," Jack said.

"Just a word to the wise, that's all," Spencer said with a smile. "Is she really your cook?"

"Just temporarily."

"Because I don't need to tell you how important it is to move in the right circles, not to lower your standards and always be aware of what impression you're making on certain people."

"Are you suggesting that Ellie isn't making a good impression?" Jack asked tersely.

"Not at all," Spencer said smoothly. "I saw the way you were looking at her. She's an attractive woman. I admit that. I just want to remind you that all it takes is one mistake to mess up your life."

"Like you did."

"In a word, yes."

"I'll remember that," Jack said. He'd remember all right. He'd remember the mess his father had made of his marriage and he wouldn't make the same mistake. He would also remember that it took two to break up a marriage and that his father refused to admit that. When Jack got married, *if* he got married, it would be a love match, a partnership of equals.

He glanced back at Ellie, looking lovely in her hand-me-down dress, a woman any man would be proud to be seen with at the symphony. How dare his father suggest he'd lowered his standards to invite her!

"Thanks for the advice, Dad," he said. "I promise I won't make the same mistake you did."

His father patted him on the back and they walked toward Ellie.

Sure, there were people here he had to talk to. Jack understood that this was only a social occasion on the surface, underneath it was all business, calculated to soften up his investors. Of course, he wasn't going to give anyone the hard sell, just subtle reminders of what this was all about. Having his attention diverted by his cook was something he hadn't counted on.

Just then Rick tapped him on the shoulder. "Got a minute? There's someone I want you to meet."

Jack hesitated a moment. He did not want to leave Ellie. He especially didn't want to leave her in the company of his father. God only knew what Spencer would say to her.

"Hey," Rick said to Ellie, his eyes lighting up. "It's you." He turned to Jack. "You didn't tell me…"

"I don't tell you everything. Now, what were you going to say?"

"Cole Hansen is here. This might be a good chance to talk to him."

Rick didn't need to say anymore. Cole Hansen was the new president of the Jeffrey Fund. Jack had been trying to get in touch with him for weeks. He'd sent him a brochure, left messages but had never heard from him. If he could get him to invest in one of his companies, it would be a real coup.

"Would you excuse me?" Jack said to Ellie. "See you later, Dad." Jack shot a glance over his shoulder and was dismayed to see his father's head bent forward, talking a mile a minute to *his* cook, to *his* date.

"So what's going on? I almost didn't recognize your date in that dress. Everyone wants to know who she is," Rick said as they made their way across the crowded room. "I knew something was going on between you two in the kitchen. I thought you didn't date the hired help."

"I don't," Jack snapped. "This isn't a date. She's a chef. My chef. I brought her because I thought she ought to see what the competition is doing. The caterer is the hottest chef in town, in case you didn't know."

"I didn't know. I do know that your chef is the hottest thing I've seen for a long time. I don't suppose you noticed?"

"Of course I noticed. I'm not blind. I'm telling you this is all about business. I'm here because I have to be. She's here because I needed a date. Why do my dates have to be the object of anyone's attention?" For some reason he'd never minded before. His dates hadn't minded, either. But he minded now. He didn't want people talking about Ellie, speculating about her. First his father. Now Rick.

"Wait a minute. Is she your date or not?" Rick asked. "A minute ago you said…"

"I know what I said. Look, I've got a lot on my mind. You know how much I'm counting on putting this deal together. If anything else goes wrong…"

"What's gone wrong? Everyone's happy. Everyone's impressed. Everyone's interested."

"I hope so. I thought you wanted me to meet Hansen. Well, what are we waiting for?" But who was dragging his feet? Who kept looking over his shoulder at his "date"? Not Rick. It was Jack who couldn't seem to tear his eyes away from her or keep his mind off of her. What had come over him?

Chapter Five

Jack met Cole Hansen and had the man's ear for ten minutes. Only ten minutes to explain his fund over the buzz of the voices in the room. But his mind was wandering. Wandering across the room to where his temporary cook was surrounded by a small group of men in tuxes and black ties. How had that happened in the space of a few minutes? He wondered what they were saying to her and what she was saying to them. Was she telling them about her restaurant plans? Was she lining up more investors in case he fell through? Or was she lining up future customers for her restaurant? Or were they just simply flirting with her? And if they were, was she flirting back? She had her back to him, and from where he stood, he had a glimpse of her legs thanks to the slit up the back of her dress. He'd have to thank Hannah for her work on the dress. It was sensational. Or more accurately, Ellie was sensational in the dress.

Jack tried to pull his attention away from Ellie and focus on Hansen and listen to what the investor said, but for some reason the words didn't make sense. People were lining up at the buffet and Ellie had suddenly disappeared from his sight. He couldn't let her go off without him. How would she know where their table was or even that they had a table?

"Nice to meet you," he blurted to Cole, before the man had finished talking. "We'll talk later." Then he pushed his way through the crowd, scanning every blonde as he went. But none of them was the one he was looking for.

When he finally found her, he put his hand on the curve of her back, just below the deep vee of the back of her dress. It was a possessive gesture. He recognized that, but she was his cook, wasn't she, as well as his date? He was paying her, wasn't he? So he had a right to feel a little possessive.

"Sorry you got stuck with a bunch of strangers," he said.

"Everyone was very nice," she said, sounding surprised. "Your father told me what a genius you are with money. That you're not afraid to take risks. Except for restaurants, of course. And in your personal life, of course."

"A chip off the old block," Jack said as a note of bitterness crept into his voice. "Did he tell you that?"

She shook her head.

"Did you tell him what our deal is?" Jack asked as he found their places at a round table set for eight.

"No, I didn't. I had the feeling he wouldn't approve."

"Of course he'd approve. He loves wheeling and dealing. Hedging his bets and trying to get the best deal. He'd appreciate your standing firm, using leverage to get what you want. As for my part in our deal, it doesn't matter whether he likes it or not," Jack said, holding her chair out for her. "It's my money."

Just then Rick came up behind him, tapped him on the shoulder and muttered in his ear. "Cole is in. Once the word gets out, everyone else will want a piece of the action. What did you say to him?"

Surprised, Jack shrugged. "I didn't have time to say much of anything."

"Maybe that's what did it. He thought you were uninterested and so cool you didn't need him."

Jack laughed. He was cool because he was more interested in watching Ellie across the room than in talking to Cole. What would his father say if he heard that his theory of all work and no play had backfired for once? He knew what his father would say. That he'd lucked out with Cole, but from now on he'd better tear his eyes away from his companion, his date, his chef, whatever she was, and pay attention to the investors he had to continue to court until they'd signed on the dotted line.

Ellie had overheard enough of Jack's conversation to know that he'd received good news from his colleague. If she didn't know it then, she knew from the change in his demeanor that things were going well. He smiled, drank a second glass of champagne and introduced her to everyone around the table as one of San Francisco's up-and-coming new chefs. He made small talk and seemed more relaxed than she'd ever seen him, except perhaps on the trampoline.

Ellie was torn between watching Jack charm everyone at the table and paying attention to the fabulous food. She studied the beef tenderloin with mushrooms, letting the red-wine *jus* roll around on her tongue, then slowly ate her potato Napoleon and braised winter greens, analyzing the flavors and filing them away in her brain.

When she looked up from her plate, she caught Jack's eye. He was grinning at her.

"Are you eating your food or examining it?" He asked, placing one hand on her bare arm and with the other hand refilling her wineglass with a 2002 Pinot Noir.

"Both," she said, her skin sizzling where he touched her.

"What's the verdict?"

"Wonderful." But was she talking about the food or about Jack? A new charming Jack, a new warm and attentive Jack who was looking into her eyes as if her opinion mattered, as if she was the most important person here tonight. She knew better, and yet…and yet…she had to admit, she was tempted to succumb to his charm. When his fingers traced a pattern on her arm, she lost her train of thought. The room spun around her, the voices faded, and suddenly there was only the two of them, alone in the crowd. She had something to say. What was it? She shifted in her chair. Oh, yes. She cleared her throat.

"Considering that she's cooking for, what would you say, a few hundred people?" she said. "It's amazing. I could never do that."

"Sure you could. With a little help. She's not back there by herself, you know."

"What do you think of the food?" she asked.

He looked deep into her eyes. "Not as good as yours."

"Really?" She smiled. She felt warm all over. Of course that could have been because of the wine. But it was always nice to get a sincere compliment. Coupled with that look in his eyes, no wonder she felt the heat radiating from her heart. "Does that mean you're going to put your money where your mouth is?" she asked lightly.

"It's looking good. For both of us." He lifted his glass and touched it to hers. "Here's to us," he said. His gaze held hers for a long moment, and suddenly all the breath whooshed out of her lungs. A sexy smile played on his lips. He was so close she felt she could see into his mind, but this time she couldn't see the wheels turning. She could only see herself reflected there. Her hand shook, and the deep-red wine sloshed in her glass.

What did it all mean? Probably that they'd both had too much to drink. First champagne, now the wine. She was vulnerable and out of practice. And he was a sophisticated man who'd seen and done it all. If she had a fairy godmother, she'd be hovering somewhere over Ellie's shoulder right about now, waving her wand to get Ellie's attention and murmuring, "Watch out, dear." Good advice.

Sure, Ellie could tell herself there was nothing going on, but her cheeks were burning and every nerve cell was alive and receptive. *Here's to us,* he'd said. He didn't mean it the way it sounded, because, she reminded herself, there was no "us."

She knew better than to take his remark seriously. He probably toasted his companion, whoever she was, every night of the week, then dumped her the next day, if the neighborhood gossips were to be believed. And Ellie was not his companion or his date. Despite his effusive description of her tonight, it was the champagne talking. In his office he'd said she was a nobody. He'd tried to take it back, but the words still stung.

Try as she did to discount it, and no matter how hard her fairy godmother tried to warn her, the toast seemed sincere and it meant a lot to Ellie. It was the look in his eyes, the tone of his voice. All of which made it impossible to look away. Partly because he was still looking deep into her eyes, while the moment went on and on. He was still holding her gaze with his as if he really meant it. But then he'd had years of practice, being the man about town, and she'd had zilch years of practice of being the object of so much attention. It was dizzying, exciting and more than a little scary.

Still, if things really went the way he said they were going, it was the beginning of the realization of her dream. If so, there was a reason for her to feel like Cinderella. Forget the prince part. She'd never looked for a prince. All she'd ever wanted was her own business. Her own restaurant. A chance to cook for people who would appreciate her food. A place for neighbors to hang out. If it was going to happen, why not take a moment to celebrate with a glass of wine and the best-looking man in the room? Where was the harm in that? It was one evening. One gala. One glass of wine on top of one glass of champagne.

When she finally tore her gaze from Jack's, she glanced at her watch. The magic moment was over.

"What's wrong?" Jack asked. "The evening is just beginning. Don't worry, the Beemer's not going to turn into a pumpkin."

"You never know, it might happen if we're not out of here by midnight," she said lightly.

The lights flickered, signaling it was time to go into the hall. As they were ushered to the fifth row center, the orchestra started tuning up.

"This is beautiful. I've never been here before," she whispered, looking up at the high ceilings, the sconces on the walls and the beautiful people in the box seats that lined the sides of the room. "So this is what money can buy." It certainly wouldn't pay to get attached to this kind of life. "Do you come here often?"

"Not really. Only for special occasions." He reached into his pocket and turned off his cell phone.

She raised her eyebrows in mock surprise. "I thought you never…"

"Only for special occasions. The orchestra doesn't appreciate electronic devices going off during the performance. Especially during Mahler's Fifth Symphony."

She nodded and leafed through her program, and there on the last page was a list of major contributors. "But here's your name. A major contributor. I'm impressed."

"That's the idea. To impress people," he said. "And it's a tax write-off."

"Whatever your reason, it's a good way of using all that money to support the arts," she said.

"Don't make me out to be some kind of philanthropist," he said. "I'm here tonight to schmooze, and it's paid off already. It looks very much like you'll get your restaurant."

"So I'll get a chance to make my dreams come true," she said. "But what will you get?"

"Me?" He folded and unfolded his program without looking at it. Ellie studied his hands, strong, well shaped and blunt-edged out of the corner of her eye. And remembered how light his touch was on her arm. She had a crazy desire to reach over and take his hand in hers. Just to share the moment. Or to encourage him to tell her what he really wanted.

Of course she didn't touch him. She knotted her hands in her lap so she wouldn't even be tempted. But what was taking him so long to answer? Finally he said, a little too offhandedly, "Just more of the same, since I've already got everything I want."

"Then what makes you keep going? What motivates you?" she asked.

"Shh," he said, putting his finger to her lips. "They're going to start."

The lights dimmed and the conductor came onstage. Though Jack took his finger away and turned his attention to the stage, her lips trembled as if he was still touching them. If a brief touch on the lips affected her so much, what would it be like if he kissed her? Thank God for the dim lights. Thank God for the distraction of the music.

So Jack didn't want to answer her question. What did it matter? The first movement was so dramatic and exciting she almost forgot about him entirely. But the third movement was lush and romantic, and she wanted to share the emotion she felt as tears filled her eyes. Intensely aware of Jack's arm resting against hers, she sneaked a glance at his profile, noting the angle of his jaw and the curve of his mouth. She had no idea if the music affected him or not. She quickly turned her head. She didn't need him or anyone to fall under the spell of the music. And she was not there to gape at her companion, the best-looking man in the hall, perhaps the best-looking man in the city.

When they emerged from the symphony hall, Jack seemed to have forgotten the purpose of the occasion—to schmooze and hustle investors. Instead he took her hand to descend the steps toward their waiting car.

"Did you like it?" he asked.

"It was wonderful. My mother used to listen to classical music on the radio. She wanted me to take piano lessons, but…"

"No time? No money?" he asked kindly.

She nodded.

"Your pumpkin awaits, Cinderella," he said, and

squeezed her hand. She turned to smile at him, grateful for his insisting she come tonight, grateful for his understanding, and most of all for his behaving as if she were the only woman in the hall.

She was floating on the arm of someone who could easily pass for Prince Charming, at least on the surface, after an incredible evening. She noticed the gaggle of paparazzi on the sidewalk snapping pictures and turned around to see who was being photographed, then realized it was her and Jack.

"I don't understand," she said, still seeing spots in front of her eyes as they pulled away. "Are you that famous?"

"Not me, it must be you," he said with a grin.

"Oh, sure. I can just see the headlines—Cook's Night Out."

He laughed and put one hand on her thigh. She sucked in a sharp breath. The warmth of his hand sent a spiral of desire shooting through her. She told herself to get a grip. It was nothing. She was relieved when he took his hand away. Yeah, sure she was.

The truth was, she was disappointed. But in the comfort of the heated leather seats and the soft music that surrounded them, Ellie tilted her head back and closed her eyes. She didn't know what to say. Didn't know who was supposed to thank whom for the evening. Didn't know if she was supposed to ask him in or if he'd kiss her. She didn't even know what she'd do if he did.

"Well," he said, pulling up in front of her house. "It's past midnight. Your dress hasn't turned to rags, and the car is still intact."

"It's late," she said abruptly and unnecessarily, and reached for the door handle. Before she could open it he'd come around and was there helping her out of the car. "Thanks for inviting me." Now go home before I say or do something I shouldn't.

He walked her up to her door. She fumbled for her key. He braced his arm against her door.

"Thanks for coming with me," he said. "I owe you."

She turned around, and he was inches away from her. His face was half in shadows, and he looked mysterious and a little dangerous. A little? He was very dangerous to her well-being. He had way too much power. The power to make her dream come true. The dream of her restaurant, of course, nothing more.

She could feel the heat from his body, smell the rich red wine on his breath and the masculine scent of his skin and his hair. She swallowed hard. What was wrong with her? She'd had a taste of the way the other half of the world lived, and it had gone to her head. A new dress, an evening among the rich and beautiful, a few glasses of champagne and she was wanting things she couldn't have, making wishes that couldn't come true.

This was a man who'd never loved anyone, and most likely never would. Furthermore, it was her best guess that he'd never been loved, not the way a child should be, nor a man, for that matter. She knew what it was like before her mother died. The feeling of being cherished. He'd never had that feeling nor did he want it. He didn't even know what he'd missed.

"Good night, Jack," she said. But before she could turn back to the door, he'd leaned forward and kissed her. Just a good-night kiss. But she wobbled on her sandals nonetheless, and instinctively put her hands lightly on his chest to keep from falling over. He took that as a sign of encouragement and pressed them tightly against his chest. She felt his heart pounding in time with hers. Then he kissed her again. She didn't expect such tenderness. Such a light touch, a hint of what might come later. It was merely a brush of his lips against hers. Heaven help her, she wanted him to kiss her again. And he did.

He nibbled at her lips, slowly, tantalizingly, coaxing them apart so he could touch his tongue with hers. She stifled a moan in the back of her throat and put her arms around his neck, wanting more but not wanting him to know. Of course he knew. He delved deep into her mouth with his tongue and it took her breath away. Her whole body was on fire. She couldn't, wouldn't stop him. She wasn't in danger. After all, on the lighted porch, how far could this go?

When he pulled away, she got her answer. She

took a deep breath. So this was his method. Always leave them wanting more. And she did want more. She longed for more. She ached for more. But she'd die before she'd ever admit it.

"Thank you, Jack," she said, proud of how even her voice was. "I had a lovely time." Very deliberately she turned, grabbed her keys and opened her door. When she closed it behind her, he was still standing on the porch, looking surprised. What did he expect? That she'd invite him to tumble into bed with her the way every other woman did? Immediately she knew that wasn't fair. She had no idea who he'd tumbled into bed with. She could only guess.

She was shaking. It took a half hour in a hot bath before she could stop. In her terry cloth robe she peeked out the front window. She half expected to see a pumpkin at the curb. There was nothing. His car was gone.

What next? Act normal tomorrow and for the rest of the week. Pretend nothing happened. Nothing *had* happened. Not to him. He'd taken his cook out for an evening on the town because he needed a date. He'd kissed her good-night a few times and most certainly had forgotten about it on the way home.

She'd do well to do the same. But it was different for her. She was an impressionable woman. She didn't date single millionaires. She didn't date anyone. She didn't kiss anyone. She didn't wear sexy black dresses and drink champagne. She didn't go to the symphony and sit in the fifth row.

No wonder she felt like her world had been turned upside down. No wonder she tossed and turned trying to put the images out of her mind, the glitter and the glamour, the flashbulbs, all the attention and the kisses. And the music. The incredible music. She lay in bed and read the program notes. The romantic part that had caused her to be so moved was called the Adagietto and was written as a love letter to the composer's wife. What would it be like to be loved that way?

Ellie couldn't believe Jack was at her door at seven the next morning. His eyes were bright, indicating that he'd slept well, whereas she felt as if she'd fought her demons all night long. And lost.

"I didn't expect you so early," she mumbled, aware that her hair was still uncombed, that there were dark smudges under her eyes and her breath was far from fresh.

"I was afraid you'd oversleep," he said, giving her a long look. Probably horrified to see what she looked like the morning after. "And I knew blueberry pancakes were on the menu this morning."

"Oh, of course. Give me a minute." She left him standing in her living room while she splashed water on her face, brushed her hair and teeth and grabbed a pair of khakis and a T-shirt. So much for Cinderella. Back to the kitchen. Back to work. Back to real life.

They didn't talk on the way to his house. Jack was busy on his cell phone, taking one call after another. It was as if last night had never happened. She took her cue from him and said nothing, not that she had an opportunity to say anything. All the while her brain was churning, trying to make sense of it all. Trying to pretend it hadn't happened. None of it. Not the symphony or the kisses on the front porch.

Somehow she made blueberry pancakes that were light and fluffy and served them with homemade maple syrup and a rasher of bacon. She *was* a professional. After breakfast, the guests went to Silicon Valley to listen to the CEO of a successful company Jack's firm had funded.

The house was quiet at last. While she sat in a kitchen chair and stared at the sinkful of pots and pans, the phone rang. It was May.

"Well, Miss Social Butterfly, I can't believe you're in the newspaper today."

"What? Where?"

"Splashed all over the society page. Who do you think you are? You don't belong there. We do. You never would have met Jack Martin if it wasn't for Hostess Helpers. You're a cook. That's who you are," May said without waiting for an answer. "And that's all. Where did you get that dress?"

"I…someone made it for me. How does it look?"

"Well…it looked pretty good. Even mother said so. Did you say it was homemade? I thought you were working this week. This doesn't look like work. April and Mother and I had to do a whole dinner party by ourselves last night while you were out on the town. And you never even told us. We had to read about it in the paper. Mother wants you to come back right away. We need you."

"I can't, May. It may not look like work to you, but it was just part of my job here. I had to fill in for someone who didn't show last night."

"Oh, that must have been a real hardship. Going to the symphony gala in somebody else's dress. With somebody else's boyfriend. And being written up in the paper. Now everyone wants to know who you are. Who Jack Martin's latest flame is. As if."

"No, they don't. No one cares who I am. That's ridiculous."

"That's what it said. It said you were the mystery woman. How does it feel?"

"It feels weird. Maybe I looked glamorous last night for once in my life, but life goes on and I was up at six today and I just made breakfast for twenty people. Does that sound glamorous? And now I have to start the preparations for lunch and dinner. They have high expectations and I'm getting paid. A lot. It's a lot of work, but it's just for one week.

You'll have to get along without me for once. Is that so hard?"

"It wouldn't be hard if everyone did their part," May said, "but last night Mother expected me to stay in the kitchen slaving away, doing your job, while she and April served. First I burned the rice, then I ground the coffee too fine so the filter didn't work and there were grounds in everyone's cup. It was awful. They threatened not to pay us. And by the way, I followed your recipe for veal cordon bleu but it didn't taste right. You must have forgotten to write down some secret ingredient."

"Why would I do that? Here's my secret ingredient, May. It's tasting. About the veal…and any other recipe, you have to taste as you go along, and it really never turns out the same way twice. I'm sure your version was just as good as mine."

"That's not what they said."

Ellie sighed. So much for trying to pump up her stepsister. "Goodbye, May. I've got to get back to work."

"You haven't heard the end of this," May said. "Mother won't take no for an answer. When she saw your picture in the paper, she was very upset."

Ellie hung up, then ignored the mess in the kitchen to go in search of the morning newspaper. She walked through the quiet house, admiring the polished oak floors, the leaded windows and the solid, comfortable leather chairs and ottomans. Jack took all this for granted. He'd been raised with money. Raised without love, according to him, but with plenty of creature comforts. Not that she'd trade her early years with a loving mother and father, but Jack didn't seem to have missed much. Or had he?

He had good taste, she had to admit that as she noted the seascape painting on the wall, so realistic that the boats in the scene seemed to be bobbing in a small bay. She checked the round mahogany table in the foyer, but there was no paper. The door to his office was open, and she glanced in. There was a *Wall Street Journal* on his desk, but no local paper. There were no pictures or mementos around except for a model sailboat that looked as if it had actually seen action. Was it Jack's? The man who'd had no childhood? Where did Jack, who was brought up in a sterile condominium, find to sail a toy boat?

He must have had toys. One of those nannies had surely provided him with balls and blocks and maybe even a toy sailboat. Or maybe it was his father who'd given it to him. From what Ellie could tell, his father was very proud of him.

But then, you never knew about other people's families. Look at hers.

Chapter Six

As if on cue, the phone on Jack's desk rang and after a brief hesitation, Ellie picked it up. Sure enough, it was for her.

"What's going on there?" her stepmother asked.

"Work. Work is what's going on," Ellie said. "I have three meals a day to prepare for a crowd of demanding eaters here with no help. I don't suppose you and the girls…?"

"Are you out of your mind?" Gwen demanded. "We've got a full schedule. I don't know how you can even ask. We're just as busy as you are, if not more so."

"Then you'll understand that I don't have time to chat right now, Gwen. Bye."

Feeling proud of herself for standing up to Gwen, Ellie left Jack's office and went back to the kitchen.

Ellie had just scanned the menu for the dinner and taken the prime rib from the subzero refrigerator when she remembered she had to give an account of the evening to Hannah and Clara.

Hannah answered on the first ring. She'd already seen the picture and the article in the paper.

"You looked beautiful," Hannah said. "Clara and I were thrilled. We cut out the picture and we have it on the refrigerator door. How was it?"

"It was wonderful," Ellie said, and began to fill her in.

"And Jack?" Hannah prompted. Did he behave himself?"

"Of course." Ellie didn't want to ask what that meant. It could mean anything from getting drunk and hanging from the chandelier to seducing Ellie on her front porch.

"You looked stunning in the dress. Did Jack say anything?"

"He wanted to know where I got it. He couldn't believe that your sister made it for me in one afternoon. I can't thank you and Clara enough."

"Oh, yes, you can," Hannah said. "In fact, you already have. How's the dinner coming?"

"I have the prime rib in the roasting pan. I'd better get busy with those duchess potatoes."

"Let me know if I can help."

Ellie put the conversation out of her mind while she chopped vegetables and sautéed mushrooms for the sauce. If she didn't concentrate on the food, she'd make mistakes. She couldn't afford to let her emotions get in the way of the food.

It was important to put emotion into cooking, if it was the right kind. If it was love, all the better. If you didn't love the person you were cooking for, at least you could love the food itself or the act of cooking it. So she thought about Jack as she rolled out the pastry for a berry pie. She thought about the music last night, and the warmth of Jack's arm against hers as they shared the experience. And, just as she'd instructed May to do, she dipped her finger in the sugar-cinnamon mixture and tasted, and despite herself, thought about Jack even more.

In Silicon Valley, Jack was thinking about Ellie. He was trying to concentrate on the lecture, but he'd already heard the same speech once before, and he wasn't in the mood to hear it again. So he sat in the back row and stared straight ahead, fixing his expression to one of rapt attention while his real attention was on his replacement cook.

The images of her formed a kaleidoscope in his mind. Just when he thought he'd seen every facet of her—from casual to sophisticated, wearing a sexy dress or barefoot in the kitchen—she surprised him this morning by appearing tousled and looking as if she'd just gotten out of bed.

Had he planned that? Was that why he'd gone to her place earlier than he'd said? Or had he just been too restless, too impatient to see her again? He didn't know. He only knew he'd been blown away by the sight of her at seven o'clock and that he'd had an almost uncontrollable desire to call in sick, forget about work and take her back to bed. To roll around on the wrinkled sheets, making love to her and spending the day that way, with his cell phone turned off. He could just imagine what his colleagues would think if they knew. They'd never believe it. They'd think he was losing his mind. They might be right.

He didn't even know how she felt about him. If he threw caution to the wind and seduced her, would she even go along with it? She'd probably look at him as if he were crazy for suggesting a day of hot steamy sex instead of a hot, steamy kitchen.

But he'd been tempted. That's how far gone he was. On the busiest day of the busiest week of his life he was contemplating making love to his employee. How crazy was that? Yes, he must be losing his mind. That's what his father suggested when he'd called this morning.

"Are you out of your mind?" Spencer had asked.

"Taking your cook to the symphony. You're going to put ideas in her head."

"What kind of ideas, Dad?" he said, clenching the phone so tightly his knuckles turned white. "That she deserves a night out? That she's a beautiful, desirable woman who just happens to also be a superb cook? Let me tell you something. She didn't want to come. It was her night off. If it was up to her she would have spent the night at home with a good book. She was doing me a favor by going with me. I needed a date. She was good enough to help me out. I owe her big-time."

"Of course you don't owe her anything. She was having a good time," his father said. "I could see that. It's too bad about the picture in the paper. Have you seen it?"

"No, I haven't."

"Well it gives the impression that you two are an item. And that's what the writer thinks, too. You've got to be careful, Jack. Women are not like us. They jump to conclusions. They make assumptions. We can't give them any ammunition. Also, everyone wants to know who she is. What do I say?"

Say she's the most interesting and sexy woman I've met in a long time. Say I can't get her out of my mind. "I don't know. Say whatever you want."

"How does she feel about having her photo splashed all over town and the writer speculating that she's your latest squeeze?" his father asked.

"I don't know. She hasn't even seen it as far as I know. And neither have I. She'd probably prefer her name not be linked with mine. Can you blame her?"

"We're getting off the subject. What I'm trying to say is that I don't want you to make the same mistake I did. When I met your mother…"

"Never mind, Dad." Jack didn't want to hear anymore about how his mother had deserted them.

"Let me finish. When I met your mother, I fell head over heels in love. I thought she felt the same about me. I thought we were in it for the long haul, through thick and thin, richer or poorer…" His father's voice shook. Jack had never heard him get emotional about his marriage, about anything actually. He didn't know what to say.

"I don't have to tell you that it didn't work out that way," Spencer continued. "She left me. Not that I completely blame her."

What? Jack was shocked. His father actually taking some of the blame for the breakup?

"I thought I'd never get over it," his father continued. "I thought I'd die from the pain. I'm only telling you this because I don't want you to get hurt the way I was. Don't ever let yourself fall in love like that. You think it will last. You think it will be forever, but there are no guarantees."

"Dad, it was just one date. I'm not falling in love." But how did he know? How did he know what falling in love felt like? "Anyway, thanks for the advice. I'll…I'll keep it in mind."

From the back row of the conference room, it was easy for Jack to sneak out without being noticed. In front of the building he bought a newspaper from a machine and quickly turned to the society column. Yes, there they were. He rocked back on his heels. She was dazzling. Seeing the photo made him feel as if he'd been slammed against the wall. Was that it? Was that what it felt like? It was almost the way he'd felt when she opened her door to him last night. Shock and surprise at the transformation, enough to take his breath away. And it was happening again just by looking at her picture in the paper.

It was the dress. It was her smile. It was the memory of the touch of her skin and the taste of her lips. He wanted to see her, he wanted to touch and taste her again. But how? Not with a houseful of investors hanging around.

He folded the paper in two, but not before he caught an ad for the Big Top Circus on the back page. For Children of All Ages, it said above a picture of a whole line of elephants parading around a ring.

He walked up and down the street, with the paper jammed under his arm, thinking about elephants and peanuts and popcorn, thinking about Ellie, her childhood and her stepmother and her stepsisters, and then he turned and walked back to the building. In-

side, he made a few phone calls and an announce-
ment to the group before he headed back to his house.

When he burst into the kitchen, Ellie was at the
butcher block slicing potatoes.

"Hold everything," he said.

She dropped her knife. "What happened?"

"There's been a change of plans. Can you save the
dinner until tomorrow night?"

She looked down at the pile of potatoes. "Sure, I
guess so. Why?"

"Something came up. The group has a chance to
visit the tech museum tonight. Special guided tour
just for them. So I made a reservation for them to have
dinner at Grimaldi's in San Jose. That way they don't
have to drive up here and back. Didn't make sense."

"Does that mean I get the night off?"

"In a way." He had to stifle his smile. He couldn't
wait to see her expression when he told her what he
had in mind.

She studied him with narrowed eyes. "In what
way?"

"In the way that you don't have to cook. But that
date you had with a good book? Not tonight."

"Don't tell me you need a date again, because I'm
not going to Grimaldi's."

"Neither am I," he said.

"But aren't you supposed to be showing them a
good time?"

"I don't always do what I'm supposed to do," he said. Oh, yes he did. He always did what he was supposed to do. But that was the old Jack. The new Jack was full of surprises. He surprised his father, he even surprised himself, and now he was going to surprise Ellie. "For example, I have two tickets to the circus tonight." He reached into his pocket and held them up in front of her.

She braced her hands against the butcher block, her brown eyes wide with surprise. "What?"

"You heard me. We're going to the circus tonight. Don't try to get out of it, because I'm paying your salary and your time is mine. Unless…it's not just for kids is it? They'll let us in, won't they?"

"Sure, of course. But why? Why you? Why me? Why now?"

"Because I've never been before, and you like the circus. I'm trying to make up for lost time. And I may never get another chance. So put the food away, Cinderella. Go home. I'll call a cab for you and I'll pick you up at six."

She didn't say anything. She seemed to be stunned. But she dutifully wrapped up a chunk of meat and a pile of potatoes and stored them in the fridge. Then she took off her apron and hung it on a hook on the wall.

"I'll take your silence as a yes," he said at last. Dammit, couldn't she show a little emotion, a little excitement? Did she have to act as if this was part of her job? Of course, maybe she'd gotten that idea from him. "This was your idea, you know, that I've missed something," he reminded her.

"I know," she said. "I'm just trying to adjust. A few days ago I was stuck in a kitchen every night and most days, too. Not that I minded. I love what I do. But last night I went to a symphony and tonight I'm going to the circus. I'm just a little…confused." She reached for her sweater and ran her hand through her blond hair.

"You're confused? How do you think I feel? Never mind. Don't answer that. Let's just say we're taking the night off. It doesn't happen that often, not for me, and apparently not for you. I can't even pretend that it's part of my job. I don't think it will do my career one bit of good to go to the circus, but…"

She stood there waiting for him to finish his sentence, but he didn't. He had no idea what he was going to say, if anything.

"But it might be fun?" she suggested at last with a little smile.

"It damn well better be fun," he said, grinning at her. "Because it might be the first and last time I do something spontaneous."

Ellie had no trouble finding something to wear to the circus. A pair of jeans and a jacket would do fine.

No fancy dress required. There would be no photographers there to take their pictures as they left the big tent. She told herself not to read too much into this rash decision of Jack's. She told herself not to read *anything* into it. She didn't understand him. She didn't need to. All she needed to do was to work for him for one week and get the money to start her restaurant.

If she had a good time doing it, all the better. If he enjoyed her company, fine. Just so she didn't enjoy his too much. Just so she remembered who she was and who he was and that falling in love with your boss was never a good idea. Not that she'd ever fall in love with Jack Martin. Where did that idea come from? She barely knew him, and what she knew was so far from what she wanted in a man it was ridiculous.

If she fell in love it would be with a family man. Someone who'd be there for her through thick and thin, to supply the support and the love. Of course she wanted passion, too. She wanted to be swept away. With all those requirements, no wonder she'd never found Mr. Right. He'd be someone who appreciated her for who she was, not Cinderella, not a scullery maid, either. Just her. Just Ellie. Someone who wouldn't forget her so fast when she was gone.

She didn't want someone who'd never had a family or a childhood. She and Jack would make a terrible pair. Never mind. She was getting ahead of herself. This was a one-time thing. An evening at the circus. Tomorrow things would be back to normal. Ellie in the kitchen. Jack wherever it was he was supposed to be, attached to his cell phone. And soon she'd be busy with her restaurant and have no time for nights out at the symphony or the circus. Restaurant owners were on duty 24/7. Relax, she told herself.

The big top smelled like sawdust and popcorn and big animals. The earthy smell brought back bittersweet memories of when she'd gone with her parents years ago. Another lifetime. The front-row seats were even better than the ones she and Jack had had last night. And what a difference in the audience! There were kids everywhere, laughing, jumping out of their seats, clapping and stuffing their faces with food. There was noise and loud music. She sneaked a look at Jack out of the corner of her eye, wondering what he thought. She hoped she hadn't hyped it too much, or he'd be disappointed.

When he turned off his cell phone, she shot him an inquiring look and he shrugged.

"I wouldn't want to disturb the performers," he said. "Or the audience."

Then he craned his neck to look up at high-wire artists tiptoeing back and forth high above them. Next he looked down at the clowns who were tossing balls in the air and catching them behind their backs. In ring three there were tigers performing with a trainer. The action was nonstop. Ellie craned her neck back and forth, afraid to miss anything. She didn't see the lone sad-faced clown who was riding around on a unicycle, until Jack nudged her and pointed to him. The clown got off the cycle and did a juggling routine so silly she laughed. So did Jack. It was almost like the trampoline, the two of them laughing together. She felt light-headed and giddy.

"If you ran away and joined the circus, what would you be?" Jack asked her.

"Me? I'd love to fly through the air." She pointed to the trapeze artists above them.

"Not afraid of heights?"

"Yes, but I could get used to it. What about you?"

"I'd be a clown. Hiding behind all that paint, I could act anyway I want and not worry what impression I was making."

Jack waved to a vendor, and in a minute they both had a pink cotton candy cone in their hands. Perched on the edge of her seat, she watched Jack put a blob of pink spun sugar into his mouth. "Like it?" she asked.

"Not bad," he said, licking his lips. "So this is what I've missed all these years."

That and a few other things, she thought taking a mouthful of cotton candy. Before she could lick the sugar off her lips, Jack leaned over and brushed her mouth with his, leisurely tasting her lips with his tongue. "Hmm," he said with a gleam in his eye as he pressed his sticky lips to hers. "Very sweet."

He wasn't talking about the candy, not in that tone of voice. She knew she should turn away and break the contact, but she was stuck. Stuck to his lips. She put her hands on his shoulders as the memories of last night's kisses came rushing back. Surely if she pushed, if she shoved, she could break away, but she didn't. Neither did he. Instead he deepened the kiss, turning it into one of spine-tingling excitement instead of just lighthearted fun. She felt feverish now, her pulse accelerating wildly as he kissed her and she kissed him back.

What did everyone else think? She could only hope no one noticed the couple in the front row kissing as if there were no tomorrow. But there was a tomorrow. And tomorrow after that.

That realization made her gather her willpower and finally pull away. She turned deliberately toward the third ring, hoping he wouldn't notice how the color flooded her face, and she tried to focus on the tigers who were jumping through rings of fire.

"I hope no kids saw us," she said breathlessly.

"Yeah, that's the kind of thing that turns kids toward a life of crime."

She slanted a quick smile in his direction. "You know what I mean."

"I don't think I do. Let me guess. Was it this?"

With one hand he gripped the back of her head to hold her steady and wrapped the other around her waist. Then he slanted his mouth and plundered hers yet again. This time she felt his tongue slide into her mouth and mate with hers. She felt as if she was slipping into a deep hole and that she might never get out. The worst part was, she didn't want to. The background music faded, the shouts, the laughter all disappeared, and the only sound she heard was her own heart pounding in her ears.

This time he was the one to break away first. No explanation, no smart remarks, he just looked around as if he didn't know where he was or what he was doing there. As for her, she was left feeling lost and alone. Ridiculous.

"Great circus," he said under his breath. "Nonstop action. We've got to do this more often."

She looked around as the world came back into focus. The tigers were still jumping through hoops, the clowns were still parading around the ring, and muscled men were swinging from ropes high above them. Kids were still screaming, and no one gave the two of them a second glance. She breathed a sigh of relief…or longing…or was it something else? Regret? For what? That the kiss was over?

"You didn't tell me," he said.

"About what?" She stared at the clowns, trying to focus, afraid to meet his gaze. Afraid he might see how the kiss had affected her, turned her bones to jelly and made her heart race. Afraid she'd see nothing in his face to show he'd been affected in the least. Not the way she had. "Tell you that cotton candy sticks to your lips?"

"Tell me your lips would stick to mine when you kissed me."

"Wait a minute. You kissed me first."

"Don't apologize. You couldn't help yourself."

"That's right. No apologies. You're irresistible. I couldn't help myself."

He grinned. "You don't have to say that just because you're working for me. Flattery isn't in the contract. But kissing, that's another matter. You read the fine print, didn't you?"

"Not exactly," she admitted. "Was there something about kissing?"

"Something? It was everything. Never mind. Then I have to assume that display of affection there had nothing to do with your obligation to me and was purely based on my animal magnetism?"

"You can assume whatever you want," she said, fanning herself with her program. It was warm in the tent and getting warmer by the minute. "Okay, so I kissed you, but I felt I had an obligation…"

"To return the favor."

"Well…"

"Anything to boost my ego, is that it?"

"You don't need me to do that."

"I need somebody. Ego boosters are hard to come by these days. My father's never exactly been the ideally supportive parent."

"What would he say if he knew you were at the circus?"

He laughed. "He'd say I'd lost my mind. He's not the circus type."

"I didn't think you were, either."

"I wasn't, but now that I know about the sideshow, I might come every night." He nudged her in the ribs. "If you know what I mean. That is, as long as you come with me, of course."

He didn't mean it. It was just banter. Then why did her heart speed up like an out-of-control race car? Because she was hungry for compliments, for flirting, for kissing and more. Because she was hungry for fun and excitement and laughter. She hadn't lost her childhood the way Jack had, but she'd lost her adolescence. Instead of hanging out in the mall with friends, she'd been at home cleaning and cooking. Instead of flirting with high school boys, she'd been in the library doing her homework. That's what she was making up for. If that was possible all in one night.

"Fortunately the circus is only once a year," she said, damping down her emotions. "Otherwise I'd lose my job. When I have my restaurant…" She stopped. She didn't want to sound overconfident.

"Go on."

"I'll be busy every night."

"Don't call *me* a workaholic."

"I didn't."

"No, but you were thinking it. Every time I get a call on my cell phone, you have that look on your face that says, 'Oh, no, here he goes again.'"

She widened her eyes, trying to look innocent. "Like this?" she asked.

"No, like this." He did an imitation of her looking down her nose with unmistakable disapproval at him. She laughed. It occurred to her that since she'd met Jack, she was laughing more than she had in years.

Chapter Seven

Out in the cool night air they walked hand in hand in easy, companionable silence to the parking lot. Like a couple, Jack thought. Like a couple who'd acted silly, laughed and kissed and had a wonderful time. They *had* had a great time, but Jack didn't want to be part of a couple. He knew what it entailed. Obligations. Commitment. Problems. He'd had experience. Only once, but the memories lingered. And they weren't pleasant ones. He'd vowed then that he'd never get entangled again. After a stormy breakup, recriminations and bitterness had followed. But right now he wasn't worried. He'd learned his lesson. He'd never fall again. Tonight? It was a one-night deal, right? Why should he worry?

If he'd temporarily lost his mind, so be it. Part of him even hoped he wouldn't find it anytime soon. He was having too good a time. Way too good. He felt like he'd been given a second childhood, or rather a first, since he'd never had one the first time around. He felt like running and jumping and doing a summersault like the clown he wanted to be. It was the circus; it was taking the night off; but most of all it was Ellie. He loved hearing her laugh. He liked seeing her cheeks flush and he liked having her small warm hand in his right now.

"How did it compare?" he asked. "Was it as good as you remembered?" What he really wanted to know was how did he compare to any other man in her life. How crazy was that? Jack Martin worried about the competition? Nobody would believe it.

"It was better. Of course, I was in the front row."

"And you were with me." He squeezed her hand.

She slanted a smile in his direction, and he felt a strange pressure around the region of his heart. He must have OD'd on cotton candy.

"Which part did you like best?" she asked.

"The clowns, followed by the tigers. No, wait, it was the elephants. You thought I was going to say the kisses, didn't you?"

"No," she protested. But he could see her cheeks flush under the lights in the parking lot.

He grinned at her. "Truthfully? I liked it all. It was

great. I had no idea a circus could be so exciting. I didn't know what I'd missed." I had no idea *you* could be so exciting. Oh, come on, he knew. He'd known the first minute he'd set eyes on her. He'd known then she was special. He hadn't wanted to turn her down.

When they got in his car he switched on his cell phone. There was a huge list of missed calls. Damn. So much for a night off. He should have known he couldn't get away with it. He played his messages.

The first, second, third and fourth messages were all from the members of his group. Their van had broken down on the freeway and then had been hit from behind by a speeding car. Two women were shaken up, the rest unhurt, and they needed to know where to go, how to get home, what to do. The voices were shaky, hesitant, worried, upset.

"What's wrong?" Ellie asked, hearing him muttering under his breath.

"Everything. I should never have turned off my phone. There's been an accident. In the van coming back from the museum." Jack ran his hand through his hair and started his engine. Then he hit the freeway, one hand on the steering wheel, the other holding his phone pressed to his ear.

When he finished, he turned to Ellie. "I'm going to San Jose to pick up the people who are stuck there. I'm sorry. I'll call a cab for you so you can go straight

home from here. Otherwise it might be a long night."
"Here" turned out to be a big hotel just off the freeway. Before Ellie could say anything, he'd parked,
jumped out of the car and told the concierge to get a
cab to take her to San Francisco. He paid the concierge, then briefly said good-night. She looked
stunned. But what did she expect? That she'd go with
him? He had no idea how long it would take or if he'd
have to fill up his car with the others.

Jack's mind was spinning. He should have been
with the group. He should not have taken the night
off. He'd shirked his responsibility, and now he was
paying the price. He consoled himself that no one
was seriously hurt. At best, they were inconvenienced
and the incident had put a crimp in his plans. This
was his fault. No, he couldn't have prevented the van
from breaking down, but he might have stopped them
from being hit from behind. He would have known
who to call and gotten help sooner.

He drove away from the hotel with the image of
Ellie in his rearview mirror, standing in front of the
hotel waiting for her cab, her face blank. He was
sure she didn't blame him. But he blamed himself.
He hoped she didn't think he'd dumped her there so
the group wouldn't see he was out with the hired
help. That was the farthest thing from his mind. All
he wanted to do was to get them all back to San Francisco and to their hotels.

They were spread out, some at a fast-food restaurant, more bored than annoyed, the ones who'd been slammed into on the freeway were at the emergency room at the local hospital, waiting to go back to their hotel after having been checked out and given clean bills of health. And still others had gotten themselves back to the city on their own.

For the rest, Jack made calls and hired cabs, and by two o'clock in the morning, he finally arrived at his house, strung out, overstimulated and dead tired. He wanted to call Ellie to make sure she'd gotten home all right. He couldn't get the picture out of his mind of her standing alone in front of the hotel waiting for a cab. What a way to end an evening.

He'd learned his lesson. He'd let down his guard and acted like a kid at the circus and what happened? He'd blown it. There was an emergency, and if he'd been there, he could have smoothed everything over. Presumably no one would even have been disturbed. He would have commandeered another vehicle, avoided the accident, and the group would scarcely have been aware that anything had gone wrong.

But he hadn't been there. He was out enjoying a second childhood, which he couldn't afford and didn't deserve. And which he certainly didn't need. Oh, he'd had a good time. No doubt about that. He couldn't remember when he'd had such a good time. But was it worth it?

Someone might have been seriously hurt, or he might have compromised the success of this project. What if some members of the investment group were so upset, they'd leave early without making a commitment to his projects? What if the rest stayed on, but then decided not to put any money into the fund? The reasons may or may not have anything to do with what happened tonight. He could only speculate.

What he did know was that he was not going to act like a kid again. He'd swerved from the straight and narrow, and look what happened. He was lucky because it could have been worse. There could have been some real injuries. But on the way back, most of the group were uncomplaining and in good spirits. No one blamed him. But Jack blamed himself.

He went to the kitchen and stood in the middle of the quiet, spotless room. What was it about a kitchen that made him want something he couldn't have? The smell of bread baking, a soup simmering on the back burner, the presence of a woman. Certainly such things weren't memories of the past. He'd never had them until Hannah had come into his life. Soon Hannah would be back, and things would be right. He wouldn't miss Ellie then. Not at all.

Ellie should have known the new and improved Jack, the Jack who forgot he was supposed to be all work and no play, was too good to be true. That man had disappeared as soon as he'd turned on his cell phone. That phone had become a symbol of what he was: always busy, always on call, always somewhere else. At least, part of him was somewhere else. Of course she understood he was needed. Of course she understood there was an emergency and that he was good at coping with emergencies. And she knew how much he had at stake.

So what was wrong with her? He didn't owe her anything. He'd taken her to the circus; they'd had a great time. They'd laughed and eaten and kissed, and then it was over. But she wanted more. She was greedy and that was not good. It was counterproductive.

Over and over she'd told herself that all she wanted from Jack was the money for her restaurant. How was he supposed to get the money if he didn't put his work first wholeheartedly and without distractions like going to the circus? His doing his job well meant she'd get her restaurant. It was as simple as that.

If only there wasn't this nagging question at the back of her mind. Why couldn't she have gone with Jack to take care of the stranded people in the group? She might have been able to help. Obviously he didn't think so. Was it because he was reluctant to be seen with her? Not likely, since he'd taken her to the symphony, and her photo was all over the paper. Or was he just being considerate by letting her go home in a cab, not knowing what was going to happen? She wanted to believe that, so she did. But she wondered...

When she got home, she found a message on her machine from Gwen. She said May was sick with the flu and they had a tea to cater the next day. She didn't beg, she didn't order, it was something in between. She appealed to Ellie's sense of loyalty to come and help out.

Ellie sighed. If she did it, it would mean breakfast for the group, ditto lunch, then do the tea across town at the yacht club and back for dinner at Jack's.

The phone rang. She knew it would be Gwen or April and she had to have her answer ready. But it was Jack.

"I didn't wake you, did I? I wanted to be sure you got home all right. I'm sorry about dumping you that way. I hope you understand."

"Of course. Was everyone all right?"

"Yes, but it was a near miss. They're lucky no one was hurt. I should have been there."

"What could you have done?"

"I don't know. Something. The point is I wasn't there."

"You were taking the night off."

"I don't have nights off. Or vacations. You know what I mean. Anyone who runs a business knows that. Whether it's the investment or the restaurant business. You take one night off and you're sunk. Because there's always someone who's willing to work harder than you are, and they're the ones who'll win."

"I didn't know it was a contest," she said stiffly. She didn't need to be lectured about the restaurant business and having a work ethic. Especially when she was contemplating a full day tomorrow and it was already almost 2:00 a.m.

"It is a contest. Between you and the next guy. If you don't know that now, Ellie, you will soon."

It was the first time he'd called her Ellie. It made her realize the magic was gone. Their relationship was strictly boss and employee, or if things went well—investor and investee.

"Thank you for the information," she said. "I'm quite aware of what a commitment running a restaurant is. And I'm prepared to make it. I'm sorry you weren't on duty when you should have been. I might remind you, it was your idea to go to the circus."

"I know that. I'm not blaming you. I'm blaming myself."

She sighed. "I haven't got time for this, Jack. I have a big day tomorrow and I have to get some sleep. Don't come by for me tomorrow. I'll be there at seven." She hung up before he could protest.

From now on it was strictly business between them. He said he didn't blame her for the lapse in his work ethic, but she thought maybe he did. After all, she was the one who'd told him about the circus. She was the one who told him he'd never had a childhood. He was trying to prove he could make up for lost time. There went that theory. Oh, well, she'd tried. And she'd had a good time. She thought he had, too. Maybe that was a good way to end it. If there was anything to end.

The next morning she told April and Gwen she'd fill in for May. They didn't sound surprised or particularly happy about it. After all, that's what they expected from her. That's what everyone expected from Cinderella. That she'd do her duty. That she'd put in the extra time and wouldn't let anyone down. After all, wasn't that what she was doing for Jack?

Hastily, running on pure adrenaline, she put out a buffet breakfast for the members of Jack's group— scrambled eggs with chives and cheddar cheese in a chafing dish, hot biscuits and homemade strawberry jam. Fresh orange juice and coffee. From what Ellie could see as she filled the chafing dishes on the sideboard in the dining room, the group seemed a little subdued that morning, but who could blame them? And maybe she seemed that way to them, too. If they'd noticed her, which they didn't seem to. Never mind, she was used to being the invisible one, the one in the kitchen. That's why the night at the symphony had been such a shock. A nice shock, but one she'd better get over fast.

She only caught a glimpse of Jack once in the dining room. He was talking earnestly with a few of the men, and he looked so incredibly fresh and wide awake and sexy, his dark hair curling damply as if he'd come straight from the shower, he took her breath away. How did he do it, when she'd barely had the energy to dab on some lipstick, run a brush over her hair and throw on a pair of stretch pants and a sweater? At the moment she felt like she was running on one cylinder. She'd never let it show, especially not to him, after what he'd said about the restaurant business. She wanted to exude energy, and self-confidence. But it was hard after only a few hours' sleep with a full day ahead of her.

Back in the kitchen, she poured herself a cup of coffee and caught her breath. She'd only made breakfast for twenty, but she felt as if she'd just run the Bay to Breakers Race across the city of San Francisco.

She had to admit, seeing Jack had sent her pulse into overdrive. The fact that he was so unattainable probably had something to do with his attraction for her. That must be it. Hopefully no one suspected. Especially not Jack.

When he finally appeared in the kitchen, she hopped off her stool and started chopping celery. She wouldn't give him reason to lecture her about the energy it took to run a restaurant. He mustn't even guess she was the slightest bit tired.

"Great breakfast," he said.

She smiled brightly. "Thank you. By the way I'll be gone for a few hours after lunch."

"Gone? Where?"

"I have to help Gwen and April with a tea. May got sick and they need me."

He scowled. "I need you. I'm paying you. Three meals a day and a tea, too? Isn't that too much, even for you?"

"What was it you said, no nights off, no vacations. I'm in the food business, Jack, and there's always someone who's willing to work harder. So I'd better get used to it, don't you think? That is, if you're still thinking of investing in me."

He walked across the room, stopped inches in front of her and looked into her face. "Of course I am. But you look tired." Damn, why hadn't she taken the time to apply some blush on her cheeks this morning? She hated it when someone said she looked tired. It made her feel defensive.

"I'm not tired," she insisted, her chin up and her shoulders back.

"Let them get someone else," he said, his face so close to hers she could see the lines etched in his forehead. Was he worried about her or about his own dinner?

"If they got someone else, they'd have to pay her. And who would they get? Who would do what I do?"

"You think you're irreplaceable?" he demanded, gripping her shoulders tightly, his blue eyes shooting daggers.

"Today I am. Don't worry," she said, taking a deep breath as the warmth from his hands traveled toward her heart. "I'll have everything ready to go before I leave for the tea. And I'll be back in plenty of time to do the dinner. It's a standing rib roast. I'm making the sauce this morning. It's a snap, believe me. The least labor-intensive of all the meals, and it will be delicious, I promise."

"I don't doubt it for a minute. What worries me is that they're taking advantage of you," he said.

"Maybe. But I left them in the lurch this week because of you, so I kind of feel like…"

"So blame me, but don't go."

"I have to go. I told them I would. This is ridiculous. You won't even know I'm gone."

"I'll know," he muttered, and he dropped his hands. "How are you getting there?"

"They're picking me up in the van."

"Take my car."

"What?"

"You heard me. I'll be here all day. Take it."

She could just hear April and Gwen when she showed up in Jack's car. The snide remarks, the sly looks, the outrage, the envy.

"No."

"You can leave when you want to," he said as if she hadn't spoken. "They can't hold you hostage, and I know you'll be back in time."

"Jack, they're not criminals."

"I'm not too sure. I think they'd kidnap you in a minute, if they could, and force you to work for them again. I saw them. I'm a pretty fair judge of people, and I want you to be on your guard. I can't afford to lose you."

She laughed. April and Gwen kidnapping her?

"You laugh. But I'm telling you to watch your back around those three."

"Only two of them today, so I'm not worried. For one thing, I'm bigger than they are."

He gave her a long, leisurely gaze from the top of her head to her running shoes. The kind of look that caused her to feel like he was touching her everywhere his eyes went, scorching her skin as he went, then he nodded and handed her the keys to his car.

He might be right. Gwen and April might take their time about cleaning up after the tea. This way she could leave when she had to. Let them talk about her. Let them give her a bad time about using her boss's car. They might be so grateful for her help, they'd hold their tongues and forgo their normal criticism. She could always hope. "If you're sure..." she said, closing her palm around the keys.

"Sure," he said.

She turned back to the chopping block. "Thanks. Now I've got work to do, Jack." Maybe he wouldn't say anything about last night. What was there to say? He didn't have to tell her it was a one-time-only happening. He didn't have to tell her he was sorry he'd gone, or sorry he'd let her off so unceremoniously, or...

"I just want to say I enjoyed the circus."

"So did I." She picked up the cleaver. "See you later."

"Also, you should take the car tonight when you finish up. Then I won't have to drive you home."

She dropped the cleaver. He was trying to avoid her. She didn't know why that hurt so much. "Or pick me up in the morning."

"Right."

She told herself he was simply being considerate. And extremely generous. How many men handed over the keys to their expensive sports car? He could have told her to call a taxi. She picked up her cleaver and started chopping with a fervor. But he didn't leave. He just stood there watching her.

"Was there something else?"

"The breakfast was great. Whatever happens, I want you to know your food has been superb."

"Thank you." She paused. "What's going to happen?"

"I don't know. That's the problem. I just don't know."

Chapter Eight

Jack was basically kidding about Ellie being kidnapped by her stepfamily, but he spent the afternoon worrying about her, anyway. He didn't know what was wrong with him. He had plenty of other things to worry about, as he'd hinted to her. He was either on the phone or in the seminar, schmoozing and trying to get a feel for how everything was going. When he saw Ellie return and park his car in the driveway, he breathed a sigh of relief.

He didn't rush out the front door to greet her, as he was tempted to do, didn't ask her how it had gone, he just watched her from the window walk around the house to the back door. Just knowing she was back made his tense muscles relax. He even felt different about himself, the project and the world. All because Cinderella had walked into his life? It didn't make sense.

More likely, it was just that he now knew dinner was on track. Because he had a creeping feeling that nothing else was. Like the success of this seminar, for one thing. He sensed something was wrong. He couldn't put his finger on it, but something was out of whack. It might have to do with last night, or maybe it was that the projects he'd lined up didn't excite the group. Whatever it was, he was worried.

When the teenagers came to help that evening, he made sure they knew they had to stay until every pot and pan was washed. He didn't want Ellie stretched to the breaking point. And he didn't trust himself to go into the kitchen after dinner. He had to stay away from her. He had to stay focused on the project, just in case there was something really wrong. Or was it doomed before it had begun?

He did the same thing the next day, hanging out with the participants and watching Ellie out of the corner of his eye. By the end of the week, he felt as though he'd been put through a ringer and hung out to dry, as Hannah would say. And that was before he got the word. The word was no.

Not one of the twenty odd members of the group was putting any money into his projects. Neither was

Cole Hansen. Had he lost his touch? Had he picked the wrong people or the wrong projects? He didn't think it was the end of the world, but his father did.

"You were distracted," Spencer said on the phone. "I saw it at the symphony. You were with that woman. This is her fault."

Jack slammed the door to his office shut. He didn't want anyone, especially Ellie, who was still in the kitchen, overhearing this conversation.

"She had nothing to do with it," Jack said. Fortunately his father knew nothing about the circus. What if he suspected Jack intended to give Ellie the money, anyway? If he knew that, he'd be sure Jack had gone over the edge. Jack didn't know when he'd decided to do it. Was it the night they'd bumped heads? Was it when their lips had stuck together or when he'd tasted her crab cakes?

It didn't matter when or where, he was going to do it. He had to do it. It wasn't her fault the deal hadn't gone through, it was his. She deserved to get her restaurant. He'd stayed away from her for the past few days to give her some breathing room, and now he wanted to be part of her life again. Only a small part of her life, of course, just on the periphery. First, he wanted to see the expression on her face when he told her that she could have her restaurant.

"What now?" his father asked.

"Now? I'm not sure. I'm looking into some new

ventures. Back to work. I've got some new ideas. But first I'm taking the weekend off."

"What? That doesn't sound like you. You haven't been yourself lately. Maybe that's why…"

"Maybe. But now is not the time for postmortems. I did my best. It's time to move on." Move on, yes, but to where? One place he wanted to avoid was his office downtown. Being out of it for this week had made him feel free.

Jack hung up and opened the door to his office.

In the kitchen, Ellie was hanging up her apron.

"Good news," he said.

"You got it?" she asked, her eyes wide.

"We got it. Thanks to you."

"But I didn't hear anything." Her nose wrinkled. God, she was cute when she was puzzled. "I mean they all just left after breakfast. No cheering, no celebrations?"

"Oh, you know, it's old hat to most of these guys. A million here, a million there. You win some, you lose some."

"What about you?"

"Me? I'm going to celebrate with you. We're going to look at locations for your restaurant. You said you wanted to be on the water."

"Well, yes, but…"

"Then let's go."

She looked as if she'd been shaken by a minor earthquake.

"What's wrong? Didn't you have faith?"

"I was afraid to. I didn't know how things were going."

"You never do with these things. I've got the classifieds here," he said, waving the newspaper in his hand. "What about South of Market, on the Bay. It's being gentrified, but there might be bargains to be had."

Ellie took her jacket from the pantry. She was dazed. After a half week of being ignored by Jack, she'd all but given up any hope of turning him into a normal human instead of a human calculator, not to mention getting her restaurant. She'd filled in for May more than once. April and Gwen had pummeled her with questions. Back at Jack's house, she'd cooked, but he'd stayed out of the kitchen. The girls across the street helped out, but Jack had been conspicuously missing. And now it was over. And yet it wasn't over. Not between the two of them. He was her investor.

Now he was here, and they were going out looking for a location for the restaurant. She felt like Rip Van Winkle, asleep for a long time, and finally waking up to a new and different world. A new and different Jack, anyway. "Well, sure, South of Market would be great, if it's not too expensive."

They ripped out the classifieds from the paper, then drove all over town, not just down by the Bay, but out at the ocean, too. Ellie was dressed in her usual, casual jeans and sweater, but darned if she didn't feel like Cinderella all over again, getting her wish at last.

They poked around vacant warehouses, investigated abandoned storefronts, looked into bona-fide restaurants for sale. There were so many, but nothing caught her eye. Nothing spoke to her. Nothing said, This is it. This is yours.

"See anything you like?"

"I like them all, but…"

"But you don't love them. You shouldn't settle for less. Let's keep looking."

They grabbed a crab cocktail on the wharf and ate from plastic cups while sitting on a small wooden bench facing the water. Fishing vessels and pleasure sailboats bobbed around in front of them.

"You asked me once what I wanted," he said, draining his bottle of spring water.

Surprised, she looked up at him. Surprised he remembered she'd asked, and more surprised that he'd tell her.

He pointed to a trim little boat with the name Mary Ann and San Francisco on the hull.

"A boat?" she asked. "Why don't you get one?"

He shook his head. "Too much work. Too much upkeep. No time to sail. Impractical."

Not too surprisingly, this from a man who'd grown up without toys.

"You have a model boat in your office."

"That's about as close as I'm going to get to having a boat. I can look at the model and dream, but I won't be tempted to sail away and never come back."

She raised her eyebrows. "You're afraid you might do that?"

"No, of course not." He got to his feet and pulled her up. "Let's go. I have a gut feeling we're getting close to finding the right restaurant." And that was the end of Jack's baring his soul to her, which left her with mixed feelings of regret and sadness. She would get her dream, but he wouldn't get his. She planted a smile on her face to cover her feelings, because she knew Jack wouldn't have wanted even a hint of sympathy from her.

It turned out Jack's gut feeling was right. They were only steps from the restaurant of her dreams. It was a tiny little fisherman's shack between two big buildings where an old guy behind the counter sold fresh fish. They almost missed the place.

They stepped inside. There was sawdust on the floor and it smelled, not unpleasantly, of fish. Ellie looked at Jack. He looked at her. Something transpired between them. She wasn't sure what it was. A kind of understanding. A mutual agreement. Her heart fluttered. Was this it? She bought a whole flounder and asked the old salt behind the counter how business was. He shrugged. She walked around the shack, her heart pounding with anticipation, admiring the view from the dirty window, picturing picnic tables, food served family style to hungry tourists and locals.

Then she and Jack walked outside and stood on the sidewalk.

Jack grinned at her. "I can tell by the look on your face. This is it, isn't it?"

"But what if it's not for sale? And if it is, what if it's too expensive?" she whispered. "He's old, maybe he's tired of working, on the other hand…"

"I'll do the negotiating," he said. "You stay out here."

"But…"

She peered in through the window, watching Jack and the man talk. Jack handed the man his business card, and they shook hands. It didn't take long.

"I think we've got ourselves a deal," Jack said when he joined her on the sidewalk.

She jumped up and down and hugged him. His arms went around her, and he kissed her on the lips. She clung to him, her skin feverish, her heart thundering. It was because of the restaurant. Of course it was. Out of the corner of her eye she saw the fish seller standing at the window looking out at them. "Uh, we're being watched." Reluctantly she pulled away. "Are you sure about this?" she asked.

"Never sure until we get an agreement signed on

the dotted line," he said briskly, apparently unaffected by their public display of affection. "But it looks good. You were right. He's tired of working. But his family didn't want him to sell. So he's going to tell them how much we're offering."

"How much are we offering?"

"Let's talk about it later. I have to go to the office, write up the offer as well as our agreement and see about some other business."

"I'm sorry, I've taken up too much of your time."

"I owed it to you. You bailed me out this week. I'll have our bookkeeper draw up a check for you today. I can bring it by. Are you free for dinner tonight? We should celebrate."

"If you want to come to my house, I could make something."

"Aren't you tired of cooking? Stupid question. Would shrimp puffs be on the menu?"

"They could be."

"You're on," he said with a grin, and shook her hand.

Jack dropped Ellie at her apartment. Before he drove away, he watched her climb the stairs to her door. As she went inside, she turned to look at him. It was as if they were connected in some physical way, by a cord or an invisible wire. There was a little smile on her lips that sent a rush of longing through him so strong he almost parked the car and went after her. He wanted to continue where they'd left off. He wanted to hold her, to feel her breasts pressed against his chest, to plunder her mouth with his tongue with no audience around and no time limit.

Hugging and kissing her in front of the fish shack today didn't satisfy him. He wanted more. All it had done was send his libido into overdrive. But for now, he knew he had to put some space between them. Just enough to let her catch her breath. But not too much space. Just until dinner, when he'd take her breath away again.

Reluctantly Jack drove away. He had the feeling he was standing on the edge of a cliff, in danger of falling over into a deep canyon that he'd never climb out of. What had he done? He'd told her he'd only invest in her if he got his capital, which he hadn't, but what difference did it make? It was coming out of his pocket, one way or another. He could afford it. He wouldn't have to sell the house or declare bankruptcy, but what had made him do it? He'd never done anything like this before.

As he'd told her, he didn't take chances in his private life, and he didn't take chances like this in his professional life, either. Banking on an unknown. Betting on a really risky venture like hers.

He wasn't pleased or particularly surprised at his father's arrival at his office, but he wished it could have waited until he was done drawing up the offer to buy the fish shack. He already knew what his father would say. So he wasn't going to tell him what he'd done. He shoved the papers aside and greeted his father.

"What happened?" Spencer asked his son, as he closed the door behind him and took a seat facing Jack's desk.

"You mean the seminar."

"Of course I mean the seminar. Everything was going so well. Everything looked good. Then bang, it was all over."

Jack shrugged. "It happens."

"Not to me. Not to you. It was that night in San Jose, wasn't it? Where were you when the accident happened?"

"As it happens I was only a few miles away," Jack said as calmly as possible.

"The question is why weren't you with the group?"

"I'm not a babysitter."

Spencer stood and gaped at his son. "That's your answer?"

"That's it." Jack managed a half smile, which only enraged his father.

"This has something to do with that woman, doesn't it?" he shouted. "Haven't I told you…"

"Yes, Dad, you've told me. Don't mix business with pleasure. But you never told me what I was missing."

"Missing? You'll be missing out on your future if you keep this up."

"You think so? Maybe I don't want the same future you have. Maybe I want a different life than you had."

"You're making a big mistake if you choose a woman over your own interests."

"The same mistake you made?" Jack asked.

"Yes, if you want to know."

"I'm sorry, Dad. I never realized you'd suffered until now. And I appreciate your advice. I really do. But this is my life. Ellie is an exceptional woman. She came through for me when I needed her and now I'm coming through for her. I'm using my own money to help her start her own restaurant."

"What? That doesn't make any kind of sense. Are you in love with her?"

"No. Yes. I don't know. Love has nothing to do with it. All I know is that I have to do it. I *want* to do it."

His father shook his head. "I hope you don't lose everything. And I don't mean the money." Spencer turned and left but not before Jack saw a suspicious sheen of moisture in his father's eyes. His father crying? What was the world coming to?

Jack sat in his chair, twisting a lead pencil in his fingers and staring out the window at the cars on the bridge without seeing anything.

Was his father right? Had he made a horrendous mistake? If he had, it was his to make. His money to lose. His woman to love. Love? He wouldn't know love if it hit him in the face. He had no idea how it felt. But just for the record, he'd like a shot at it before he was too old. One thing for sure, he didn't want to end up bitter and alone like his father. Oh, Spencer would never be poor, and no other woman would ever take advantage of him. He'd made sure of that.

Jack tried to concentrate on work. He talked on the phone, sent messages, wrote up a report. At five o'-clock he walked out to the lobby. Mary, the receptionist was just leaving.

"Did my father leave?"

"Yes, Jack. He walked out with the blond woman who came to see you."

Chapter Nine

Jack felt like he'd been kicked in the gut. "No one came to see me."

"Well, a woman was here, but after she talked to your father, she said, 'Never mind.'"

"Oh, God," he said.

"I'm sorry. I should have called you."

"It's all right. There was nothing I could have done."

But there was something he could do now. He drove to her house. He knocked on her door. And waited an eternity for her to answer while he worried that she had left the country, gone to start a restaurant in Tijuana. If he only knew what his father had said to her, then he could be prepared. When she finally came to the door, he heaved a sigh of relief. She hadn't gone anywhere. Not yet. She looked pale and composed, and that scared him more than if she'd been hopping mad, screaming and carrying on. But that wasn't her way. There was no smell of food, no warmth in the house. So much for dinner. That invitation was obviously canceled. The atmosphere in her house matched the look on her face.

"You lied to me," she said, her lips barely moving as she said the words. "The deal fell through."

"Yes, but it doesn't matter. It wasn't your fault."

"It was my fault for taking you to the circus that night. That did it, didn't it? Your absence turned the investors off."

"I don't know. I'll never know. It's over and done with. It's time to move on. Anyway, it was my idea to go to the circus," he said. "I made the choice, not you. Now I'm offering you the money out of my pocket, just like I'd planned."

"*If* you'd gotten the deal. You didn't. Well, it's my choice to turn down your offer. We had a deal. I knew what I was getting into. You're offering me charity and I won't take it."

"Why not? I thought you wanted this restaurant more than anything."

"Not more than being lied to. What kind of a business relationship is based on a lie? Don't answer that. I don't want to know how you do business. I heard quite enough from your father."

"What did he tell you?"

"Nothing that I already didn't know. Except for the part about the deal falling through. He said you're a chip off the block, that you're a workaholic and any woman who fell for you would be out of her mind."

Jack laughed mirthlessly. "What did you say?"

"I assured him he had no worries on that score. That our relationship was strictly business."

"So you assured him you are not interested in me in any way except as a potential investor."

"No, that's wrong. I'm no longer interested in you as anything at all," she said, as bright spots of color appeared in her cheeks.

"I don't get it. Why won't you take my money? What have you got to lose?"

"My self-respect."

"You think you'll lose your self-respect by taking my money to start a restaurant?" he asked incredulously. "It's the same money as before. What's the difference?" But he knew what the difference was, and he realized now he should have told her the truth. But the result would have been the same. She would have turned him down. If it hadn't been for his father…

"There's a big difference and you know it. You yourself told me you were not in the business of investing in restaurants. You said I was doomed."

"That was before I knew you. Before I knew what a great cook you are and how determined you are."

"Yes I am. And I'm determined not to let you give
away your money on something you don't believe
has a chance of success. Now if you'll excuse me…"
She looked down at his foot which he'd planted
firmly in the doorway. "I'm not going to argue with
you anymore."

"And you're not going to invite me in, either, are
you?" he said. If she would just give him a chance
to explain. If she'd give him a chance to tell her how
he felt about her. That is, if he *knew* how he felt
about her. But the look on her face, the way her
nose was scrunched up as if she'd smelled something bad told him this was not a good time. When
would be a good time? Tomorrow? The next day?
Or when he figured out how he felt and what he was
going to do about it. He didn't know, but he knew
he had to keep trying. There was too much unre-
solved stuff between them to walk out of her life
like this.

"Okay," he said as calmly as he could while damping down the storm brewing in his head, while stifling all the things he wanted to say but couldn't.
"We'll talk about this later."

She opened her mouth to say something, but she
didn't. It was just as well. He didn't want to hear her
say there was no point in talking about it now or later.
He didn't want her to shut him out of her life before
he figured out what part he wanted to play in it.

"Wait," he said as she was closing the door. "What are you going to do now?"

"I'm going back to work. I'm going to save my money and when I have enough I'm going to start my own restaurant. By myself. On my own terms." Her eyes were blazing as she closed the door, no, slammed the door in his face. The only thing he could do was to leave.

He'd just started the engine of his car when his cell phone rang. He was not in the mood to talk to anyone, especially not his father. But sooner or later he'd have to. As much as he wanted to, he couldn't avoid the man forever.

"You think I'm interfering in you life," his father said.

Jack heaved a sigh. What could he say? "It's all right, Dad. Let's forget it happened."

"I can't. I've been thinking. Just because I made mistakes, doesn't mean you have to. It's too late for me to change, but not for you. Anyway I have to apologize."

"It's okay, really. She would have found out sooner or later."

"Nevertheless, I want to make it up to you."

"It won't do any good. She won't listen to me and she won't listen to you. She's very proud and she wants to do things her way. Let it go."

"Of course, if that's what you want."

"That's what I want." Jack hung up and drove away.

* * *

Ellie stood at the window watching Jack drive away. She blinked back the tears. Thank God he'd left before she started to cry. He would have gotten the wrong idea. The idea that she was suffering. Of course she was sorry the restaurant fell through, but she was even sorrier that Jack couldn't level with her. She cared about him. She wanted him to get what he wanted. But what was that? A sailboat? When she'd first asked him, he said more of the same. What kind of a goal was that?

Finding that restaurant, sharing the discovery with Jack, imagining the possibilities, picturing herself in the kitchen turning out warm chicory salad with wild mushrooms, or at the door, welcoming customers, sharing the success with Jack, counting up the night's profits with Jack. Celebrating with Jack. Those were just dreams. She'd been crazy to think they would come true. They'd all come crashing down today and that hurt. It hurt, as if someone had driven a spike deep in her heart.

Meeting Jack's father had opened her eyes. He'd told her that the deal had fallen through and, in so many words, that Jack had lied to her. Of course this was all in the guise of being friendly and helpful. But it sent her into a state of shock. She stood there in the lobby staring at Spencer Martin. Wishing she'd never come to the office. Wishing she could tune out his words. But unable to move or leave because she knew he spoke the truth.

"What can I say? Jack is a playboy. But you must know that by now. He's subject to weakness where women are concerned," Spencer said. "Can't help himself. I understand because I'm the same way. He might offer you money, but there will be strings attached, and I wouldn't want to see you get hurt. I'm no analyst, but I suspect this is due to his mother leaving. I did my best, but he can't resist a pretty face, and you, my dear, have a very pretty face, plus you fulfill a man's fantasy—food and love in one package."

"But I don't..."

"Of course you don't love him. And he doesn't love you. But people get swayed by emotion and think they're in love when they're just in lust. I know because it happened to me and Jack's mother. Take advice from an old man, and stay away from Jack. For your own good. He will try to give you money under the guise of helping you, thinking that will buy your love, or attention, or whatever you want to call it, but I can tell you are not the type to be bought."

She'd come away dazed and hurt. Of course she wouldn't take the money if the deal had fallen through. Of course she couldn't be bought. Jack knew this and yet he went along with it; he went with her, participated in her dream, acted as though it was a done deal. Why? What did he really hope to get out of it?

The next day Ellie went back to Hostess Helpers. She didn't expect a warm welcome. She didn't expect anyone to say, "I told you so," either, since they didn't know the story of her dashed hopes, and she certainly didn't expect the place to be in chaos.

Gwen barely looked up when Ellie walked in the door. If only the atmosphere in the shop matched the sunny skies outside.

"This is the thanks I get?" Gwen yelled, seemingly oblivious to Ellie's arrival. She was aiming her remarks at May, who was standing with her back to the window, arms crossed over her waist, a look of defiance on her face. "After all I've done for you."

"I appreciate it, Mother," May said, but she didn't sound appreciative at all. "But I have to make this decision on my own."

"You don't have to do anything of the kind. I know what you're doing. You're giving up. There's no shame in being single at twenty-four. Look at Ellie."

May looked, so did April who was sitting at the desk, which was piled high with bills and requisition forms.

"She has no possibilities at all, but is she giving up and settling for someone beneath her? Did she let one night at the symphony turn her head? No, she's back here to work today, just as we knew she would be."

Ellie wondered what on earth they were talking about. Of course they expected her back at work

today. But the part about no possibilities? She wanted
to step into the middle of the room and shout, "Stop!"
She wanted to tell them she'd turned down a restaurant of her own. She wanted to tell them that even
though Jack was the quintessential society playboy,
he'd taken her to the circus and he'd kissed her. And
then he'd offered her money out of his own pocket
to start a restaurant. What would they say to that?
Probably something like, "Are you crazy for turning
him down? Have you lost her mind? What were you
thinking? Now what are you going to do?"

It was good that she held her tongue. She didn't
want to hear anyone cast doubts on her sanity just
when she was wondering about it herself.

"Tell her, Ellie, tell her she's crazy," Gwen said,
leveling a steady glare at her stepdaughter.

"I have no idea what you're talking about. I just
got here."

"This one—" Gwen pointed one bony finger at
May "—wants to get married to the personal trainer
at the health club that I paid good money for them to
join." Here Gwen's gaze swept over both of her
daughters. "So they could meet someone suitable."
She didn't have to say what *suitable* meant. It meant
someone with money. She turned to Ellie. "Do you
know how much a personal trainer makes?"

Ellie shook her head. "I didn't know you worked
out," she said to May.

"I don't. That's what he loves about me. I'm not all muscled." She smiled shyly.

"But how…"

"How did they meet? Good question. Tell her, May."

"Mother won't admit it, but it was all because of her. She's the one who insisted we go to the club. I never wanted to exercise, and I still don't. Well, there I was trying to figure out the stupid treadmill machine when Danny came over to help me. One thing led to another and now we're engaged."

"I didn't even know you'd met someone," Ellie said. "You never said anything."

"They were keeping it a secret," April said from behind the desk. "Even from me, her own sister." She frowned and shuffled the papers on the desk. "Now who's going to do all the work?"

Ellie wanted to remind them that neither of them had done any work to begin with, so why worry now, but she kept her mouth closed. She didn't want to add flames to the fire in the room.

"Enough of this," Gwen said. "Until she actually gets married, she's part of the team. Look at this calendar." She pointed to the chalkboard on the wall that was full of parties, dinners and receptions scribbled in under the dates. "Because of Ellie, we're backed up. All right, everyone, let's get to work."

And so went the week. And the week after that. Ellie went through the motions, but she couldn't help

thinking of the time she'd spent at Jack's. Instead of
taking orders, she'd been in charge. Then there was
Jack. Ellie knew she'd done the right thing by turning down Jack's offer, but there were times, like the
catered lunch right down the street from his house,
when she was up to her ears in the dough for indi-
vidual meat pies and her sisters were their usual help-
less worst. Gwen was outside having a cigarette, and
as the hour approached to begin serving and the pies
refused to brown, Ellie's stomach was in knots from
nerves. She wondered if maybe she'd been a little too
hasty in refusing Jack's generous offer.

There were good days, too, mostly the ones with
children's parties scheduled, when she knew she'd
done the right thing. When the kids were so cute and
so appreciative that she lingered longer than she was
supposed to, telling stories and playing games. It
was probably the closest she'd ever get to having
kids of her own, so why not enjoy them?

Another week passed, and she was in the office by
herself, taking bags of shrimp out of the freezer in
back to make a paella for a fiftieth birthday party in
Diamond Heights, when a man walked into the office.

"Anyone home?" It was Jack's father.

Ellie wiped her hands on her apron. "Hello, Mr.
Martin."

"I hope I'm not disturbing you," he said, looking
around the shop.

She shook her head. "Is this about a party?"

"No, I'm afraid I have nothing to celebrate at the moment. Although one can always hope…" His mouth twisted as if he'd already said more than he intended to. "No," he continued. "I've come to see you. To apologize."

"There's no need to apologize for telling the truth," she said stiffly.

"But I wasn't exactly telling the truth," he said. "Or rather, I didn't know what the truth was. Oh, it was true the deal fell through. Jack lied to you about that. But the part about why he lied, well, I jumped to conclusions there and I'm sorry."

"Excuse me?" Ellie's knees were so weak she had to sit down in a swivel office chair. She had no idea what the man was talking about. Or why he was there. Nothing made any sense.

"What I'm trying to say, and probably getting it all wrong, is that I was mistaken about Jack. I don't understand him or why he's doing what he's doing. He's not like me at all. Just when you think you know your children, you find out they've grown up and you don't know them at all. And what's worse, you have no control over them."

Gwen would agree with you on that. He sounded so sad, Ellie felt sorry for him.

"I'm sorry for any inconvenience or misunderstanding I may have caused," he said, and then he left

before she could say anything else or ask him what
he meant or how Jack was.

She went back to work, totally confused as to the
purpose of Spencer Martin's visit. Now, besides the
cooking and the shopping and the planning, she was
doing the billing, as well. Gwen was too upset over
May's engagement to drag herself out of bed most
days. In a way Ellie appreciated the freedom to do
things her way, but she needed help badly. Most days
she got April and May to help her, by bribing them with
the promise of catering their weddings. Though April
still hadn't met Mr. Right, she was encouraged by
May's success. As for May, she was so much in love,
she'd even agreed to be a clown at a birthday party on
Saturday for which Ellie would be her usual Cinderella.

But Saturday afternoon May was late. The pizza
had been delivered and devoured by a dozen little
seven-year-old boys and girls followed by cake and
ice cream. They'd played games for an hour, and
now it was time for the clown. Where was she? May
had never been a clown, so Ellie didn't have high
hopes for her performance, but Ellie had coached
her and provided her with a wheelbarrow filled with
prizes. Since she'd fallen in love, she seemed more
willing to act silly and wasn't so worried about looking put together. Since her fiancé thought she was
perfect as she was, it was a big boost to her ego, and
she seemed like a different person.

May was busy planning her wedding, and since her mother didn't want anything to do with it, May had to step up to the plate and make all the arrangements. Well, except for the food, which Ellie had promised to take care of. Falling in love, albeit to the wrong person, according to her stepmother, was the best thing to ever happen to May. Now if only April could have the same good luck. As for herself, she'd already fallen in love with the wrong person. She had finally admitted it to herself after many sleepless nights and much soul searching.

She loved Jack for the motherless child he once was and the man he'd turned out to be. She loved him for the way he worked, wholeheartedly and intensely, and especially for the way he'd learned to play, on the trampoline and at the circus, with wholehearted abandon. But she did *not* love the way he'd lied to her, even though she knew now he thought he was doing her a favor.

Unfortunately he hadn't fallen in love with her. He liked her. He'd felt sorry for her. He'd offered her money and he'd kissed her. But that wasn't good enough.

Just as Ellie was about to give up, May arrived in the clown suit, jogging merrily around the manicured lawn. The children went crazy, following her as if she were the Pied Piper.

But the clown was much taller than May. The

clown suit was too short for whoever was in there. A red wig, a huge red nose and white painted face disguised the imposter. He ran much faster than May. He did a back flip and a summersault. He juggled balls in the air. He tossed presents from a huge bag and had the kids scrambling to pick them up.

Ellie stood and watched, bewitched, befuddled and bemused. This was not May. May hadn't come. May had sent someone in her place. Typical May. Getting someone else to do the work for her.

Parents started arriving in their Lexus's and SUV's to pick up their kids. The clown continued his antics. Parents stopped to watch. No one wanted to leave. Finally the clown took a bow to thunderous applause, and the kids and their parents finally left.

Ellie walked slowly across the lawn while her heart beat irregularly against her ribs. She stopped only a foot from the six-foot, three-inch clown with the broad shoulders and bright blue eyes.

"Still mad at me, Cinderella?" he said.

"After that performance, how could I be?" she asked lightly. She wouldn't give him the satisfaction of thinking he meant that much to her. "How did you get here?" she asked.

He grinned, the huge red-painted mouth tilted upward making him look even crazier than before. She giggled helplessly, in spite of her shock at seeing him.

"In my car."

"I mean…"

"I know what you mean. Can we go somewhere and talk?"

"I don't know what we have to say to each other. Except, thanks for filling in for May."

"You're welcome. Do you think there's any future for me?"

She held her breath. It was the way he was looking at her, so intense, so riveted that, try as she might, she couldn't look away, couldn't pretend she didn't understand the double meaning in his question.

"As a clown?" she asked.

"As anything. I'm looking for a new job."

"What happened to your old one?"

He took off his wig and shook his head. "Didn't work out for me."

"They didn't fire you, did they?" she asked, shocked and worried that she'd been the cause of his leaving a job he clearly liked.

"No, no. I quit. You asked me once what I wanted. What my goal was."

"You said, 'more of the same.'"

"Well now I want less of the same. No, none of the same. I've been doing some thinking these past few weeks. I want something different."

"How different?"

"I was thinking of opening a restaurant."

"What?"

"A little place on the wharf where I can tie up my boat outside."

"Your boat?" she said, feeling dazed and dizzy.

He took her arm. "Sit down," he said. "And take off those glass slippers before you faint."

She slipped off the slippers and sat on the grass breathing deeply until she got her brain in gear. It was all too much to understand. Jack here. Jack as a clown. Jack leaving his job. Jack buying a sailboat. He sat next to her. When she finally looked up, he was watching her. The look of concern on his funny face made her give him a reluctant watery smile.

"Ellie," he said. "This is going to come as a shock to you, but I'm not the same guy who hired you a few weeks ago. Something happened to me that night…maybe it was the knock on the head. That's what my dad thinks."

"He said not to believe you, not to listen to you. That you tell all the women the same thing."

"It used to be true. But then I met you and you knocked some sense into my head. Literally. But I can't have my new life without you. You and your restaurant. *Our* restaurant. I figure I can do the books when I'm not out sailing or catching fish for lunch. It won't be charity, it will be community property."

She sat there staring at him as tears flooded her

eyes, unable to move or speak. She knew what she'd always known. He was the man for her. The man she'd fallen for the first day she'd seen him. Despite what he'd said. Despite how he'd hurt her feelings. He was blunt, he was frank and he was almost always honest. And, God help her, she loved him.

He brushed a tear from her cheek with the back of his thumb. "Don't cry, Cinderella. Say something. You deserve Prince Charming, I know that. And I'm not him."

Ellie's heart overflowed with love. She leaned forward and kissed him on the tip of his red nose. She wiped her tears away and cleared her throat. "You are a prince. My prince. You're also a clown and a darn good one."

"But could you love a clown?"

"If he loved me."

"It's a deal," he said, his ridiculously silly, lovable clown face lighting up. He grabbed her hand, shook it and pulled her close. "For the rest of your life. I love you, Cinderella. With or without your glass slippers, you'll always be my princess."

"And you'll always be my prince. I love you, Jack." She choked, but the words came tumbling out. "Thanks for coming after me. Thanks for taking a risk on me."

"There is no risk. Not with you. You're a sure thing. My sure thing."

The next thing she knew, her tiara had slipped off
her head, but she had a diamond ring on her finger.
And red clown paint all over her face.

Epilogue

The opening of the new restaurant on the wharf was cause for celebration and acclaim. It was small but charming, with real fishnets hung from the ceiling, photographs of vintage sailboats on the wall and long tables where food would be served family style.

The place was packed. Jack and Ellie, who'd gotten married only a few months earlier, warmly greeted customers arm in arm at the door. May and her fiancé poured champagne. April circulated through the crowd with trays of crab cakes and shrimp puffs, smiling hopefully at any and all single men.

Ellie couldn't believe how much her stepsisters had changed since Gwen had moved to Florida to retire. May's engagement had taken years off Gwen's life, or so she said, and she didn't want to waste any more years stuck in an office or kitchen, so she closed Hostess Helpers and both May and April had new jobs.

They'd been surprised and pleased to be included in Ellie's wedding as bridesmaids. The three sisters weren't inseparable, but they were closer than they'd ever been, and Ellie was delighted they'd volunteered to help out at the grand opening.

"April, I want you to meet my fairy godmothers," Ellie said, when Hannah and Clara arrived. "They're the ones who made this fairy tale come true."

"We did our part," Hannah said modestly. "But it was meant to be. The prince finds the glass slipper, it fits Cinderella and he marries her. And they live happily ever after."

A few minutes later Ellie crossed the room with a glass of champagne in her hand to where Jack was eating a shrimp puff. "What do you think?" she asked.

"I think you're the world's greatest chef. And the most beautiful. And the sexiest." He wrapped one arm around her. "Have I mentioned I want to spend the rest of my life with you?"

"As in happily ever after? That's the way the story ends."

"For us it's just the beginning. I love you, Cinderella."

Still dazed, still dazzled that he was hers, her heart brimming with happiness, Ellie raised her glass. "Here's to love," she said. "And happy endings."

* * * * *

*And turn the page for an
excerpt from Carol Grace's
next heartwarming fairy tale,
HIS SLEEPING BEAUTY,
coming in Fall 2005 only
from Silhouette Romance....*

There it was again, the flutter of white shimmering in the moonlight. This time he was going to get to the bottom of this mystery and find out who the mysterious figure floating around his back fence was. He set his coffee cup down and strode across the damp lawn until he stopped suddenly and stared.

There under the fragrant eucalyptus trees was a woman in a white gown only ten feet away from him. Her dark hair was tousled by the breeze and her sheer gown billowed, giving her an ethereal look. Under the gown he could make out the outline of her breasts and hips. His body reacted as if he'd been given a shot of adrenaline, and he felt a sharp quickening of his senses.

She was slender, this vision, but had curves in all the right places. He tilted his head and watched as the figure moved a little closer. Who was this ghostly creature who was seemingly unaware of his presence? As he stood there, she bent over and picked up a handful of eucalyptus nuts.

"Hello?" he said.

She murmured something and looked past him as if he wasn't there. It couldn't be Mary's niece—the woman who was so shy she had to be coaxed outside—out for an evening stroll in his yard, could it? If it was, maybe she didn't know she was outside, because she was sleepwalking. Thank God he'd put a fence around the pool.

He put his arm firmly around her shoulder and gently turned her toward her house. She continued to clutch the eucalyptus nuts in her hand, but she didn't resist. He murmured what he hoped were soothing words about how he was taking her home, but she didn't appear to be listening.

Somehow he knew enough not to wake her. He'd read somewhere that it could be disturbing to a sleepwalker. So he walked her into the house and up the stairs, clumsily bumping against the polished railing on one side and her hip on the other. The first bedroom door was open and he could see a rumpled bed. She'd obviously been tossing and turning.

"Is this it?" he said more to himself than to her.

She didn't answer, he didn't expect her to, but she headed straight for the bed, as if on autopilot, put the eucalyptus nuts on the bedside table, lay down, put her head on the pillow and closed her eyes.

He stood there for a long moment wondering what to do. Did sleepwalkers walk more than once a night? If so, should he lock her in or post himself at the door downstairs? He stared down at her pale heart-shaped face, at the dark hair that was spread out on the pillow and felt totally bewildered. It didn't make sense. How could the shy, introverted woman he'd heard about have turned into an enchantress from another world? He should really leave. Go out and lock the door behind him and check her out tomorrow.

Instead he just stood there, wondering if, like Sleeping Beauty, it would take a kiss to wake her. Sure, she might jump up and whack him over the head with that vase of flowers on the dresser, but what did he have to lose? A lump on the head. An embarrassing explanation. He'd always been a risk taker. So he leaned over and brushed his lips against hers. Soft, full lips. Tempting lips.

She didn't wake up. She didn't leap up and smack him one. She smiled. That was it. Just a smile. But what a sleepy, sexy smile it was.

Was she dreaming? Or was he? Did she know what had happened? Would she remember this tomorrow? Should he tell her? Was he crazy? He pulled a blanket up to her shoulders and ran his fingers over her bare shoulder where her nightgown had slipped down. She was safe, and he realized there was nothing more he could do for her tonight.

Tomorrow he'd have to alert Sleeping Beauty that, in case she didn't know it, she had a problem. Or rather, if she kept coming to his place in the middle of the night, *they* had a problem.

If you enjoyed what you just read,
then we've got an offer you can't resist!

Take 2 bestselling
love stories FREE!
Plus get a FREE surprise gift!

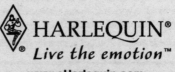

SILHOUETTE Romance ®

COMING NEXT MONTH

#1778 THE TEXAN'S RELUCTANT BRIDE—
Judy Christenberry
Lone Star Brides

Thomasina Tyler had no interest in settling down. But the marriage-minded Peter Scholfield had other ideas. For this cautious beauty had captured his interest, and the mouthwateringly handsome executive always got what he wanted!

#1779 FAMILIAR ADVERSARIES—Patricia Thayer
Love at the Goodtime Café

She was the rich girl, he was the rancher's son. And now that she was back in town, the chemistry between Mariah Easton and high school sweetheart Shane Hunter was stronger than ever. But a long-standing family feud would force Mariah to choose between her family and the man of her dreams....

#1780 FLIRTING WITH FIREWORKS—Teresa Carpenter
Blossom County Fair

Mayor Jason Strong was devoted to keeping order in his small town. Only an exotic stranger with an impish glint in her eye was disturbing the serenity of his quiet community. If the handsome widower and single father didn't watch out, the sparks flying between him and the lovely Cherry Cooper might make his peaceful life explode!

#1781 THE MARINE'S KISS—Shirley Jump

Nate Dole had plenty of experience on the battlefield, but that didn't prepare him for Jenny Wright's third-grade classroom! The feisty children had the once-hardened marine thinking twice about the merits of civilian life...especially if it included stolen moments with their alluring teacher.

SRCNM0705